They're Not Crazy -

They're Southern

By Delia Duffey

They're Not Crazy – They're Southern

By Delia Duffey
Version 1.0
Release 202

DISCLAIMER

This is mostly a work of fiction; therefore, the stories and characters are fictitious and are wholly imaginary. Any public agencies, institutions, or historical figures mentioned in the story serve as a backdrop to the characters and their actions. Some of the towns mentioned are actual towns, but not necessarily associated with events.

Copywrite 2023 Delia R. Duffey

Acknowledgements, Etc.

For all the people who are not on this side to read this work and laugh – My Mama, Honeyboy, Dale Marie, Jay Koonce, Nancy Guillory, Marsha George and many others. I'm fairly sure Amazon delivers to Heaven. This is dedicated to you.

To those still on this side who were forced to listen, read, comment and critique, including, but not limited to, Lillian Terrell Peterson McElroy, Barbara Jean Bingle Hawkins and the forever young, Celeste Graves, this is for you too. Special thanks to Elise Bentley for the outstanding front and back cover illustrations.

The stories presented here have been told or heard over meals, over cocktails and in various social settings for years. At the end of each telling, someone would always say, "That is so funny. You should write that down." So I finally did.

There is an element of truth in each tale.
Sometimes it is just a fraction of the truth as in The
Night Liberace Landed In Lubbock. Liberace really
landed in Lubbock. The rest is fiction. Sometimes it
is the entire truth as in how my parents actually
met in The Wedding of the Decade.

How To Use This Book

This book should be used:

When you need a chuckle or a laugh,

As an affirmation that your family is not the only one with crazy relatives,

As an affirmation that you are not as crazy as the people in the stories, and

When you need something for a gift-giving occasion.

They're Not Crazy – They're Southern

"I'm saying this is the South, and we're proud of our crazy people. We don't hide them up in the attic. We bring 'em right down to the living room and show 'em off. See, Phyllis, no one in the South ever asks if you have crazy people in your family. They just ask which side they're on."
Julia Sugarbaker – Designing Women. Season Four, Episode Seven – Bernice's Sanity Hearing

Contents

The Ice Man Stayeth

Monday, August 2, 1937 – Colfax, Louisiana – Day One

Sheriff Leroy Givens sat down at the counter of Hooker's Café. Hooker's was the only café in town and almost everybody in Colfax dropped by sometime during the week. The café sat on the corner just off Main Street on Highway 71. The menus said "Hooker's - The Home of Good Cooking," and it was. Phinee Tumminello, owner, waitress, and sometimes girlfriend of Leroy sat a freshly brewed cup of Community Club in front of him.

"You up and out early. You here at 8:30," she said. "You usually don't show until about 9:00." Sheriff Givens took a sip of his coffee and poured some of the hot liquid in his saucer to cool.

"Had to go out early to The Quarters. Reverend Manny Pation died this morning. First I had to go to The Blue Goose before I drove out to The Quarters to tell the family. Ned Duffy sent that

Swafford kid who works for him to find me. By the time I got to the store, Ned and Clarence Faraldo was putting him the icehouse. Said he just dropped dead while loading the ice buggy. Must a been his heart."

"Already knew he passed," Phinee said. "Phoencia sent Jackson about 7:30 this morning to say his Mama and his auntee, Photenia, 9Manny Pation's twin nieces was not coming in today because they are charge of the repast. You know the big meal before the Going Home ceremony? I sent him back with a ham and told him to get a couple of chickens from my backyard next door. So, which daughter did you take Manny Pation to? Lucille or Clotille's house? Lucille's house is bigger, but her sister's is closer to the church.

"Nope. Left him in Ned's icehouse for now till the family and the church decide. They ain't no funeral homes in the parish. There is just that one that does Black folk in Alexandria. Besides nobody,

Black or White, can afford an undertaker in these times. I guess they will care for him the best ways they can. I am kinda worried."

"How come?" Phinee asked pouring another stream of brown liquid into his cup to top off his coffee.

"Today is Monday. Black folks don't do their funeralizing 'cept on Saturdays. Then they bury on Sunday morning before church services. That's a long time to keep a body cool. Ned Duffy's Blue Goose is the only store with an icehouse. Owns a cooling board too. He don't charge the families to use the cooling board. Tells folks he has two cooling boards – one for White folks and one for Black folks. But he really only has one. He usually don't even charge for the ice. Says it's just solid water." Phinee wiped the counter with a damp rag.

"Who cares what color the person is laying on the cooling board? It's a board with holes in it set on two sawhorses with ice buckets underneath to cool the dead. Dead is dead. Dead don't have a color. The family is going to cover the board up anyways with a nice tablecloth or a curtain and lay the body on top."

"I reckon the family will get him Friday.

The folks will have the going home service on Saturday and bury on Sunday," Givens said.

"That is still a lot of ice for my Uncle Ned to give away. No wonder he don't make no money at the Blue Goose. He gives everything away." Phinee walked away to take an order from the traveling salesman from Pineville. She turned it in to Gladys O'Quinn who was helping in the kitchen with Phoencia and Photenia being gone. She walked back down to Leroy's end of the counter.

Sheriff Givens looked up and said, "True. Ned is an old softie. Always wants to help folks. Say, I'm going fishing Friday on latte Lake. You want to come? I'll be back Saturday evening," he asked. He lifted the heavy glass cake cover and took a donut.

"Naw," Phinee replied, "I told Jackson to tell Phoencia and Photenia, they could use the kitchen Friday night after closing to help prepare the repast meal. I magine the church men will barbeque meats and chickens and all kinds of meats that tastes like chicken. You know they always have a big going home celebration for their passed loved ones. Lots of folks from all over Louisiana will be in town on Saturday to view Manny Pation's remains. Assuming they hold up in Uncle Ned's ice house. If Sugar Boy Thornton makes ribs, there could be all kinds of folks from all over the state. What if something happens?"

"Ain't nothing going to happen," Sheriff Givens said, "Manny Pation and his family are some of the nicest folks in the parish. I'd rather be with some of them than with lots of white trash I know from down around along the levee toward Boyce. Trash is trash. It doesn't have a color either."

Phinee walked to the cash register to take the salesman's ticket. He tossed a nickel toward her, winked and said "That's for you, Doll Face. What time you get off? " Her look could have burned

a new button hole in his vest as she said, "Thank you. I'll let my

boyfriend, the Sheriff sitting over there keep it for me" and walked

back toward where Leroy was sitting at the counter.

"I know, Leroy. Everybody for miles around loved Manny

Pation. Didn't make no difference that he weren't White. His people

were good and kind folks. He and Ida May raised all four of their

children to be hard working people. All them learned to read and

cypher. And that man could preach. I went to a couple of Going

Homes that he preached. Remember when that mule kicked Cletus

Riley in the head, and he died? It might have been that one. Heck,

remember when Manny Pation was written up in The Colfax

Chronicle?"

Leroy said "I sure do. Front page if I recall. I kept the clipping

somewhere. Not only was he the first baby born in the parish that

year, but he was also the first Black baby to be born in the state that

wasn't born a slave. Yep. He was born on January 1, 1863. That's why his Mama named him Emancipation Lincoln. Nobody could hardly say emancipation, so they just started calling him Manny Pation."

"All that is true, Leroy, but it could be a big service on Saturday. I bet lots of folks will come. It being Saturday to come to town anyway." "They ain't nothing gonna happen. 'Sides, Deputy O'Quinn can take care of anything if it comes along. Well, I best get back to work. See you tomorrow. Let me know if you change your mind about going fishing."

Sunday, August 8, 1937 – Day Six

Leroy Givens walked into a packed Sunday morning at Hooker's Café at 8:10 . The Catholics down the street from St. Joseph's let out after 7:00 o'clock mass. The Methodists and Baptists were just getting up and moving and were drinking coffee before the services. He took the only open stool at the end of the counter.

Phinee poured him a cup of coffee, waited and grinned while he "saucered" his coffee to cool. She was looking right at him when he looked up and reached for a donut. She slapped his hand before he could lift the cake cover. "You need to stop eating so many donuts. You gonna catch the sugar diabetes – not to mention get fat. You done fleshed out over your belt buckle."

It was then he noticed the café was awfully quiet. He spun slowly on the counter stool to see all eyes were on him.

"What's so funny?" he asked turning the stool back to Phinee. "And I am going to eat that donut," he said reaching for it.

"Reckon, you ain't heard," she grinned.

"Heard what?" Leroy asked. "I had a flat tire coming back from fishing. Didn't get home till after midnight."

Let's just say that Manny Pation didn't exactly go home yesterday. They didn't bury Manny Pation on Sunday."

What?" he exclaimed almost choking on the donut. "What do you mean? How do you know?" He gave her a puzzled look to see if she was pulling his leg.

Clarence and Pete Faraldo and Ned Duffy went to the repast meal. The church sold barbeque plates for a quarter a plate. There was so many people come from all around to see the Reverend laid out and pay their respects to the Reverend and his family. Some come as far away as Tioga. I told you there would be lots of folks when they heard Sugar Boy was cooking ribs. Anyways, the church made so much money they decided to put the Reverend back in the icehouse and do it again next Saturday."

"Great Caesar's ghost!" he exclaimed. "Whose bright idea was that? What were those hooligans doing going to the repast meal anyway?"

"I reckon they got invited. Manny Pation worked for Uncle Ned at the Blue Goose. Uncle Ned is the only shop keeper that lets the colored folks shop there on Saturday. Holds the store open an extra hour on Saturdays just for them. Manny Potion's daughter, Cloteel, works for Clarence at the dry cleaners. And Phoenicia's boy, Jackson kind of works for both of them and most everybody else in town. But there he is in Uncle Ned's icehouse, The Reverend Manny Pation, propped up next to a side of beef I plan to use this week."

Phinee told him her Uncle Ned stopped by Saturday evening before closing and told her that he said he was in the middle of telling the family when they could return the cooling board when Clarence and Pete jumped in. Ned said it was Clarence who suggested that since a large sum of money was raised, they could repeat the repast next Saturday and celebrate the going home then. The deacons took a vote and decided if Ned didn't mind, they thought it was a good idea since the church was always in need of money.

"So, they just going to hold him over like a matinee at the picture show at The Pink Elephant?" Phinee shrugged her shoulders.

Leroy huffed and said "Well, I guess he'll hold if the ice holds. I'm sure they will get him in the ground next weekend. I'll make sure I talk to Ned. Say, why don't you come to Alexandria with me on Saturday? I got to go to a sheriff meeting, but it's over at noon. After that we could go to Brenthurst Field and watch the Aces. It's a double header against Shreveport Sports. We get to take the Sheriff's car with the lights on it," he grinned.

By Saturday morning, Phinee was looking forward to driving to Alex with Leroy. She enjoyed being outside even in the hot August temperatures. Leroy bought hot dogs and Co-colas and they had a picnic on the tables outside the stadium.

Inside the stadium, the stands were covered but there were no individual seats. Rooters, as they liked to be called, sat on long wooden benches like bleachers. The ground beneath the stands was covered in peanut shells. Once inside, they shared a bag of peanuts and added their shells to the ground.

The Aces won the first game easily, but the second game went into extra innings. They didn't leave the ballpark until almost 7:00 to drive back. They still had plenty of time to get home before dark.

When Leroy pulled the car in front of Phone's house he said, "Somebody pinned a note to your screen door."

"Oh Lord, I hope nobody died," she said as she jumped from the car and ran up to the porch.

By the time Leroy got to the porch, Phinee was laughing so hard she could not talk. She handed the small white paper to him. In penciled hen scratch he read "Didn't bury. He's in the icehouse at Ned's. Love, Clarence."

Wednesday, August 18, 1937 - Day Thirteen

When the Sheriff stopped by Hooker's for his morning cup of coffee, he was surprised to see Walter Seymour, the Postmaster waiting for him. Phinee poured his cup of coffee. He frowned when he noticed the donuts had been moved to the opposite end of the counter.

"Morning, Walter," he said. "How come you not down at the post office putting up the mail? Is something wrong?"

"No, No," he said. "I wanted to deliver this to you by hand. Thought it might be important with it being from Baton Rouge and all." Walter handed him an envelope.

Are you sure you didn't just want to know what the letter says?" Leroy asked. Leroy looked at the envelope. It was from the Louisiana Department of Health. He took out his pocketknife and sliced open the envelope and pulled out a single sheet of paper.

Beneath the embossed letterhead saying it was from the Louisiana Department of Health and the address it read:

August 9, 1937

To Leroy Givens, Sheriff, Grant Parish, Colfax, Louisiana

It is my duty as a faithful public servant for the state of Louisiana to inform you of a public health hazard in your parish. As this is the parish of your jurisdiction, it is imperative that this issue be resolved immediately.

I refer, of course, to the disposal of the remains of Emancipation Lincoln Washington. It is my understanding these remains have not been buried and are currently residing in unsanitary and improper health conditions.

Therefore, consider this letter as a warning that if this issue is not resolved in an appropriate time frame, fines and possible incarceration may be issued to all parties involved.

This issue poses a threat to public health and must be resolved immediately.

I remain,

Your Faithful Government Servant,

Richard Perky Long

Leroy's face turned red starting at his neckline. The more of the letter he read, the more color his face took on. By the time he finished, he was almost purple. He carefully folded the letter and slid it back into the envelope. He then folded it again and shoved it into his shirt pocket opposite his badge.

"Anything wrong?" Phinee asked.

Leroy stormed out of the café but yelled "I'm going to find Clarence Faraldo. This is over!"

Friday, August 28, 1937 – Day Twenty-Six

Phinee said as soon as Leroy sat down at the counter. "There is a jackass from the government looking for you."

"From the courthouse?"

"No. Says he's from Baton Rouge, He's sitting in that last booth over there. Probably has something to do with that letter you got."

Leroy glanced toward the far booth to see a middle-aged, fat, balding man stuffing pancakes into his mouth.

"How do you know he's a jackass?"

"He works for the government. They are usually one and the same. Besides, he told me he worked for the government. In fact, he made big deal about him being related to Huey P. Long by marriage."

"Probably every jackass politician and bureaucrat in Louisiana claims kin to Huey Long. Shouldn't be a problem," Leroy said easing off the counter stool. "They buried Manny Pation on Sunday."

Phinee replied, "Before you go talk to him, you might want to know something. She watched him as he eased back onto the stool.

"What?" Leroy cried. "Clarence promised me he would not do it again!"

Phinee looked at him and grinned. "How long have you been sheriff in this parish?"

"Two years, this September 1. Why?" he asked.

"Well, you wasn't born here, so that accounts for something, but I figured you would have learned not to trust or believe anything my Uncle Clarence, or my Uncle Ned will say or do. Especially, if there is a laugh to be had."

She leaned close to his ear and whispered "Manny's in the icehouse. The church thought he would last one more weekend. Thought you ought to know that 'fore you go to talk to jackass from the government." She grinned and walked back to the kitchen.

Leroy fumed as he walked to the last booth and stood at the end of the table. "I hear you are looking for me," he said staring at the pasty-faced man.

"If you are the sheriff, then I am looking for you," the man said and belched.

"I am Sheriff Leroy Givens. To whom do I have the pleasure of speaking, and may I ask why you are looking for me?"

"Set down. I will tell you," he said wiping syrup from his chin with his tie.

Leroy sat opposite him in the booth. The man took a long swig of coffee and said, "I assume you know you I am?" Without waiting for a response, he continued "My name is Richard Perky Long. My great uncle by marriage was the great

Huey Long. I am the Assistant Director of the Division of Public Health Hazards.

I have been disposed, on behalf of the state of Louisiana, to ensure that the deceased, one Emancipation Lincoln Washington, is properly buried and is no longer a health hazard. I am staying until Sunday, and I want to witness that Negro being buried. I have a ticket on the 12:30 train back to Baton Rouge. I expect to be on it with a signed letter from you witnessing the burial. Do you understand?"

Leroy took a deep breath and said "Yep. I will see to it" and stood to leave.

"One more thing," Long said, "I am staying at the LaSage Hotel. While I am here, where might a fellow find some entertainment? Perhaps some card games and maybe some refreshments of the flesh?"

Givens stared at him and replied "You are staying at the LaSage. I am sure you will not have any trouble finding any vice you desire."

"Swell," said Long. "I shall meet you here at 8 o'clock promptly on Sunday morning to oversee the burial. I expect to be picked up and transported to the burial service to witness the event. If this individual is not laid to rest, I am authorized and prepared to file charges."

"Then I would not hang out too long at the LaSage," Givens replied seemingly unmoved. As he excited the booth he turned back and said "Say, if there is a fellow named Duffy sitting at the card table, his tell is when he touches his hat."

By Friday sundown word had spread that a government man was in town and about to shut down the going home party. It was just as well since after almost four weeks, the Reverend was beginning to look a lot like a haunt.

The church lowered the price of the barbeque plates to fifteen cents because the Reverend was beginning to spoil around the edges. The deacons figured the folks coming to view didn't need to pay so much since the Reverend was kinda decomposing.

Sunday, August 30, 1937, Day Twenty-eight

Phinee poured Leroy a second cup of coffee and took away his empty plate of bacon and eggs. It was almost 8:20. "I cannot believe that jackass from the government ask the law where to find vices against the law. I guess that is what they do in the state capitol."

Just then Phinee and Leroy watched a bleary eyed and obviously hungover Richard Perky Long flop down in the booth opposite him. So much for the Perky part thought Leroy.

"I thought you said that Duffy's tell was when he touched his hat," Long said.

"No, I said his tell was when he touched his flask." Givens could hardly keep from laughing.

"That's right. Duffy's tell is when he touches his flask. He'll take a newcomer ever time. Ain't that right Sheriff?" Phinee grinned. She refilled Leroy's cup of coffee and sat a cup and a menu in front of Long. Long shoved away the menu. "What time is this function?"

Leroy looked at the clock behind the counter. It is 8:45 now. The burial is at 9:00 I reckon we better leave."

Sheriff Givens made sure he took every hairpin curve at full speed, hit almost every pothole in the main road and did a fishtail as he turned on to the gravel road leading to The Quarters. Richard Perky Long just kept getting greener and greener.

Leroy parked the sheriff's car under a pecan tree at the edge of the church. The family was already gathering around the hole in the ground. The men acting as pall bearers were standing in front of the church ready to bring the wooden coffin. "Ain't you gonna get out so you can see better?" Givens asked Long as he got out of the car.

Long said "I can see from here." He then opened the car door and tossed his night at the LaSage on the ground.

Leroy walked around the front of the vehicle, careful not to stand too close in the event of another projectile. "But how are you going to know if the body of Manny Pation is in the box if you don't go look? They might be burying a box of rocks for all you know.

"You don't expect me to walk up that hill and look inside, do you?"
Long asked.

Leroy looked at him as said "Well, they ain't going to bring him down here."

Long stood up slowly and pulled down his vest. He straightened his tie and reset his hat on his head. As they walked the twenty or so yards to the church steps, he began to feel better. That is until the deacons opened the coffin so he could review the remains. There was not enough ice at the North Pole to take care of almost four weeks. Manny Pation was emitting an order that was a cross between a New Orleans voodoo ceremony and a whorehouse. The perfumes used to cover the decay worked overtime but to no avail.

Long turned green again and ran down the hill. He tripped over a root and went ass over tea kettle. When he stood up he lost whatever remained in his stomach. Leroy and the deacons were laughing so hard they almost dropped the coffin. Leroy watched them nail the lid on the coffin and start toward the burial site. Givens looked at Johnny Butler and handed him a fifty-cent piece. "Put that in the collection plate cause it was worth two bits to see that jackass roll down the hill."

So Richard Perky Long witnessed the burial of Manny Pation Washington. Leroy Givens signed the affidavit that made it official. Long made the 12:30 train back to Baton Rouge. Manny Pation was buried after his fourth going home and repast meal. The church made over $600 dollars.

Corduroy Watkins

I had been living at Mrs. Weaver's boarding house in Flora, Louisiana for almost a month when the first incident happened. I could tell Carl was angry when he sat down for breakfast that morning. "Dadgum it!" he exclaimed "One of you low-down, dirty dogs used my toothbrush."

"Sit down, Carl. Nobody used your toothbrush," Cecil said as he loaded four slices of bacon on to his plate. Carl took his place at the table across from me. "'Sides," Cecil continued passing the bacon to Carl. "No sane person would want to use anybody's toothbrush. Let alone one that has been in your mouth."

"Well, somebody did," Carl said in a huff.

There were only four full-time boarders at Mrs. Weaver's boarding house in Flora. There was room for one or two more, but they were reserved for an overnighter. Those rooms were usually for drummers moving through the parish drumming up business trying to make a dollar.

The full-time boarders were me, Randall, the new bookkeeper at the sawmill, Cecil who ran the commissary, Carl of used-toothbrush fame who ran the dry goods side of the commissary, and my cousin Skeeter, whose real name was Phillip, but nobody used it, who was kind of the jack of all trades. We all worked at Weaver Brothers Sawmill. I was only 23 years old, and Skeeter was a year older. Cecil and Carl were in their 30's. Cecil was just living there until summer when school let out. Then his wife and his two children would join him, and they would rent one of the sawmill houses from Weaver Brothers where the white-collar workers lived. Carl said he was a confirmed bachelor, but he sure seemed to spend a lot of free time over at the Thibodeaux house. They had four girls.

Flora was a small unincorporated town in Natchitoches Parish about 25 miles from the parish seat of Natchitoches. There was only one two-lane paved road and it connected Flora to

Highway 120. The other roads and the road to the sawmill were

brown gravel that created towers of dust when the log trucks drove

down them.

There wasn't too much to the town except the sawmill and

the pipeline pumping station. It had a school and of course a Baptist

and Methodist Church. But Weaver Brothers employed almost all

the men in town except the two town preachers, the schoolteachers

and the few that maintained the pumping station. Weaver Brothers

was the only commissary for several miles, and everybody came by

at least once during the week. It served as the Post Office, the dry

goods store, the grocery store, the meat market and the feed store.

One could buy or order almost anything needed.

There were two other boarding houses in Flora besides

Mrs. Weaver's. The one closest to the sawmill was Mrs. Nunn's and

was for single men who worked inside the mill. The other was really

just a few rooms at Miss Bessie's down in the quarters. Mrs.

Weaver's boarding house was for those who worked at the

commissary or in the office at Weaver brothers.

Mr. Weaver owned the sawmill and he and Mrs. Weaver

used their home as a rooming house. It was a big white house that

had two

screened in porches, a sitting room for visitors, and six bedrooms.

The

boarders only had one bathroom down the hall, but it was inside.

That

was better than the bathroom I had at home. That one sat about 20

yards behind the house.

The Weavers lived in a wing off from the kitchen. They

installed another bathroom just for them around 1930. There was a

big school-house clock in the foyer that gonged the time on the hour

and gonged once on the half hour. Meals were served at 7:00 , noon

and 6:00. If you were not at the table when the last gong sounded, you had to wait until the others were served. You took the chance of not getting a good piece of meat or no dessert, so everybody paid attention to the times.

In the spring and summer time, we took our meals on the front porch. It was a long, narrow, screened-in porch that ran along the front of the house. It faced the morning sun and there was usually a breeze. It was furthest from the kitchen and cooler.

In the fall and winter, we took our meals on the back porch. Most places had a screened in back porch that they called "the sleeping porch." It faced the evening sun and was near the kitchen, so it was warmer.

Mr. and Mrs. Weaver had an old hound dog named Gus that was allowed to sit on the porches when we took our meals. Everybody loved Gus and Gus knew he could always count on a treat from each of us.

"Why do you think somebody used your toothbrush, Carl?" Cecil asked.

"Cause it was wet and I hadn't used it yet. That's why. I forgot my shaving mug this morning when I went down to the bathroom. I set my toothbrush and my can of Pepsodent Tooth Powder down and ran back to my room to get it. When I got back my toothbrush was wet, and the top was off my Pepsodent tooth powder."

"Well, that's what you get for not picking up your stuff and being too far from the bathroom," said Skeeter. "Remember that time Cecil loaned that drummer his can of Pepsodent? But it was really talcum powder? He cussed Cecil for a month of Sundays." Everybody howled with laughter.

I enjoyed listening to the men around the table. I had just finished Mrs. Lynn's Business College in Shreveport. I was quick with numbers and the business college people said I had a pretty handwriting and made pretty numbers. I wanted to be closer to home, but any job in 1933 was hard to come by. Let alone one like the opening at Weaver Brothers.

It was truly an answer to my prayers. It paid $22.50 a week and because I was working at the sawmill business part, my room and board at Mrs. Weaver's was only $4.00 a week including three hefty meals.

"Still," Carl mumbled, "I can't believe some varmint would have the gall to use my toothbrush."

"I bet it was that drummer," Skeeter said loading an extra helping of scrambled eggs on to his plate. "Not the one that used the talcum power. The one that left this morning. What's his name?"

Most of the true drummers were gone by the 1930's but there were a few that still drove the countryside. My daddy had been a drummer when I was growing up. He drove a horse-drawn wagon from town to town selling lady things. He called his business

Notions Potions & Lotions. He stopped at town stores, apothecaries,

hotels, and sometimes just houses along the way. He sold sewing

notions like ribbons, threads and bobbins. He sold all kinds of lotions

supposedly to keep your skin young and beautiful. And like many

drummers he sold elixirs like Hadacal for whatever ails the body and

soul. He could sell you something for liver spots, fallen arches,

flatulence, dropsy, colic and tired blood.

Most drummers today were honest, reputable salespeople

just trying to drum up business. This of course was due to the

legislature passing Anti-Drummer laws that required men to be

licensed and pay a fee to get the license.

Mrs. Weaver was particular about the regular drummers

she rented rooms to. Most of the drummers who passed through

Flora were old timers, but if there was a new fellow, she always

demanded to see their license.

But every so often, a scoundrel would slip through. This was the case with Corduroy Watkins. His name wasn't Corduroy. It was Roy. We called him Corduroy behind his back because he always seemed to favor wearing brown corduroy pants that gave off a little whisking, swishy sound when he walked.

"The one from up around Pollock or the one from up around Cloutierville?" Carl asked.

"Yeah. Him. The Cloutierville drummer," Skeeter said stuffing a biscuit in his mouth. "He left early this morning, and he only shows up every other week," Skeeter said. "I bet he did it."

"Well, when he gets back, I am going to make him give me a quarter for a new toothbrush," Cecil said putting his napkin on his plate.

Two weeks later, Corduroy returned for his overnight stay at Mrs. Weaver's. He was a tall, thin fellow with beady little black eyes set close together. He drove an old farm truck in which he carried his trinket-filled suitcases in the back. When he looked at you, it was like two muskie dime grapes looking at you. He wore a black bowler hat with a narrow brim that set low almost to his ears. He had a neatly trimmed mustache over his thin lips. We laughed and wondered if the mustache was the reason he spoke in a winey high voice like a screech owl. He mostly sold elixirs, but the first time we all tried one, all they did was make us drunk. There was just something about him that was shady. Mrs. Weaver only rented it to him because he was her sister's husband's nephew.

Most of the time none of us took an interest in what he talked about. Mostly because all he talked about was himself. He was a legend in his own mind.

Two weeks later at breakfast, Carl arrived just as the seventh gong sounded from the clock. He sat down just as Corduroy was pulling out of the driveway. "It's him, alright!" he said.

"Who?" I asked.

"Corduroy used my toothbrush. I set a trap for him and purposely left my toothbrush and tooth power out. Of course, I used it first."

"What are you going to do about it?" asked Cecil.

"Don't rightly know. I'll probably have to have words with him. That is another 25 cents he owes me for another toothbrush."

The first week in June when Corduroy showed up at Mrs. Weaver's for supper and to spend the night, he looked at me that night at said, "I hear, Randall, that you are quite good with a Kodak camera. Is that right?"

I looked at him and said, "Well, I do have a good Kodak, but I'm not a professional photographer."

Suddenly Skeeter piped up and elbowed Cecil and Carl in the sides and said "Oh Randall, is a real good picture taker. Ain't he Carl?"

Carl looked a bit confused but chimed in with "Oh, yes. He can take your picture, for sure."

"Don't need a professional. Just need some nice snapshots of myself to share with this girl up around Coldwater. I've been courting her a little. Her Papa has some money, so I want to send some good pictures. She would be quite a catch. Of course, I would be quite a catch too." There was a round of throat clearing, snickers, and Carl just gave a loud harrumph!

"Well, I guess I could take some pictures," I smiled quizzically at Skeeter and the others. Something was up. I couldn't wait to see how this played out.

"Swell," he said and handed me a roll of film and two one-dollar bills. "Here is a roll of film with twelve exposures. After you take the pictures, mail the film to San Antonio to get it developed and have the pictures returned to the Commissary. They will be ready when I return."

We agreed that the early morning would provide the best light, so I told him to be outside the boarding house at 6:30 the next morning.

He was there right on time. He had on a black store-bought suit and a matching vest over a crisp starched white shirt with a high collar. His black tie was knotted in a full Windsor that made him look like a dandy.

Mrs. Weaver had a beautiful backyard filled with flowers growing in beds and hanging from hooks off the porch. There were steps descending from the back porch. I told him that I had selected some really nice places for him to pose in Mrs. Weaver's back yard.

First, I had him pose standing on the steps. Then I had him pose standing in the yard with his legs apart and his arms folded. I had him pose standing on one foot with one leg up. I had him pose bending forward and sticking his butt out. Within 15 minutes we were finished and made it to the breakfast table just as the hot biscuits were coming out of

the oven and as the last gong from the clock sounded. Everybody else arrived about that time too. Corduroy did not seem to notice. Mrs. Weaver was smiling as she set the plates of food on the table.

We didn't see Corduroy until two weeks later. In the meantime, me,

Cecil, Carl and Skeeter watched the mail every day to see if the pictures came. The day before it was time for Corduroy to arrive, we were rewarded when the small package arrived at the Commissary.

That evening, we all sat down for supper. Mrs. Weaver was an excellent cook, and we were treated that night to pot roast, potatoes, carrots, biscuits and gravy. As we were almost finished, I stood up and said "Excuse me. Mr. Watkins, your pictures arrived yesterday. Let me get them from my room." Carl left the table the same time as I did.

I handed Corduroy the small brown package when I returned and sat down between Cecil and Skeeter. Corduroy snatched the packet from my hands. He looked at the first print and said, "That one is not too bad." He looked at the second print and then third print and screamed "What the ...? You people did this on purpose!" He began tossing the prints on the table in anger.

"Look! There is a slop jar in every picture. This one has the three of you

monkey faces standing behind me on the back porch holding slop jars above your head. You had me raise my leg and this one looks like I am about to use the jar. This one has you standing behind me," he said pointing to Skeeter, "holding the jar and it looks like it is on my head! You didn't see it?" he screamed at me. "I want my money back!"

Skeeter very calmly said "Actually, they are sometimes called thunder jugs." Cecil said "That's true. The well-to-do folks call them chamber pots." Skeeter chimed in saying "That's right. The poor folks call them piss pots."

Corduroy's face turned from red to purple with each breath. "I know dang good and well what they are called. I can't use any of these. She will think I knew the pot was there and did it 'purpose."

"Well," Skeeter said, "you are kind of full it." Before Corduroy could respond, Carl came around the side of house carrying Gus in his arms.

"What cha got there, Carl?" Skeeter laughed yelling from the table. We all stood up to look out the screen. Gus was slobbering and squirming in Carl's arms. Just then Carl pulled his toothbrush from his shirt pocket and started to brush Gus's teeth. Gus started howling like he had just treed a coon. Carl was dancing around trying to hold him and brush his teeth. Mrs. Weaver came out to the porch to see what the ruckus was about. Carl said, "Mrs. Weaver, Dr. Morris said Gus is a fine coon dog, but he has a bad gum disease, and you was supposed to brush his teeth every day. Thank you for laying out that toothbrush this morning so I could use it on him."

Corduroy didn't say a word, but we noticed his face turned a bit pale and he suddenly left the table. We could hear him gargling the Listerine in the bathroom. Hopefully, it drowned out the riotous laughter and knee slapping on the front porch.

He was gone the next morning when we all sat down for breakfast, and nobody mentioned it at breakfast or lunch. That evening, Mrs. Weaver served homemade vanilla ice cream with fresh black berries as dessert. This was a special treat. As I filled my bowl for a second helping, she said, "Boys, that was a terrible bunch of pranks you pulled on Mr. Watkins. He will no longer be staying with us."

We all looked into our bowls of fresh ice cream feeling somewhat ashamed. Then Mrs. Weaver broke out laughing and said, "I can't thank you enough." We never heard from Corduroy

Watkins again.

Bomanicials

"Bomanicials, don't forget to weed the flowers by the garage."

"Yessum. I won't forget," he hollered back.

He laughed to himself. For almost three years, Miss May Grogan reminded him about the flowers by the garage. Every Friday as soon as he showed up promptly at 7:00 AM to do her yard chores, she hollered out the back door. "Don't forget to weed the flowers by the garage."

Every Friday he mowed what the sawmill people called grass. The front yard was mostly dust, and the back yard was mostly sticker burrs, dandelions and onion weeds. Up around the house and by the garage, Miss May's hydrangea bushes and bed of zinnias were the envy of the five other houses' occupants who lived alongside the yellow gravel driveway. She was related to most of them - two brothers-in-laws and their wives all of whom she felt were beneath her. This row of houses was where the sawmill owners lived.

Even though May had been married to Henry Grogan for almost twenty years, she insisted that he and anybody else call her Miss May. She seldom socialized among the women in the tiny sawmill town of Fostoria in East Texas. This included several of her in-laws that lived within yelling distance. Rather she drove her Cadillac to Houston or flew to New York to visit her family and friends. If she was forced to socialize in the sawmill town, she always mentioned attending an opera or a stage production or some other pretentious activity that nobody even cared about, assuming they even knew what she was talking about.

She always told people that Bomanicials had a secret ingredient he added to the soil to make her flowers bloom like they did. Bomanicials never told her that he always added fresh cow patties when he redid the flowers in the spring.

There were many things Bomanicials never told Miss May. He never told her that her husband and his boss, Mr. Henry Grogan gave him $5.00 to do the yard. She gave him $2.50. Seven bills and two bits, cash on the barrelhead, for half a day's work. That was almost white man's pay.

Three years ago, Mr. Henry saw him at the planner mill and called him over. He had just married Leola and they had just moved from deep East Texas. He had worked in the sawmills since he was nine. People had said the sawmills in and around Magnolia were higher paying. He was scared. People sometimes made-up stories about new people in town and the ones they made up about Black people were always scary.

When Mr. Henry said, "I've been hearing a lot about you," his knees began to shake.

"I heard you got ambition, boy. That right?" Mr. Henry owned the Magnolia sawmill plus he and the Grogan Brothers owned most of the mills, timber and mineral rights in east Texas. His shock of white hair and his wide girth made him a perfect example of a big daddy plantation owner.

"Yessir," he stammered.

"Heard you don't drink or gamble. Don't beat your wife. That right? Go to church on Sundays?"

"No sir. No sir. Yessir." Bomanicials was aware he was not breathing.

"Well, I told my wife I would get somebody to do her yard on Friday mornings. Can you do that? She'll fix you a sandwich for lunch, but don't expect much. Thornton over at the white commissary meat market says he has to slice the baloney so thin you can almost see through it."

"Oh yessir," he said sharply exhaling. "I shore can."

People often wondered about the marriage between Henry Grogan and the former Miss Pine Tree, May Jean Snyder of

Marshall. May Jean's father owned Snyder Industries, a sawmill of great magnitude in East Texas.

"Good," Mr. Henry said. "I want you to go mow the yard and tend to my wife's damn flowers. She'll want to pay you, but she is cheap. I tell you. I am the richest man in town, and it is my money anyway, but she divides one paper napkin between us. I'll double what she gives you. Go tell Cecil at the back of the Commissary to give you a lawn mower. He got a couple of new gasoline motor kind the other day. You can start this Friday."

"Bomanicials! I'm going to put a baloney sandwich and Co'-Cola on the back porch for you when you get hungry." For almost three years of Fridays, Miss May would yell out the back door announcing lunch. Lunch, that was his signal that Miss May was satisfied with the yard. He would eat, take his pay and go to work a half day at the sawmill. His two dollars and two quarters would be underneath the Coca-Cola bottle. One time she put the money under the paper plate but with only the skinny baloney sandwich to weigh it down, it blew into the freshly mowed back yard.

Bomanicials reached for the green glass soda bottle only to find nothing. He looked under the paper plate. No money. Did she forget? Just then he heard Miss May on the back porch. "Bomanicials, Mr. Grogan forgot to leave my daily pin money. I do not have any money. Can you come by Monday?"

Bomanicials said, "Oh, Miss May! Leona was going use the money to buy the babies shoes this weekend when the salesman come the commissary.

It would be a mighty hardship if you know what I mean." His heart was beating. He and Leona were saving for a car.

"Well," Miss May said, "I could write you a personal check, but you probably cannot cash a check, can you?"

"Oh yessum. I can cash a check," he replied. "We can cash

checks from certain people down at our commissary in the quarters." He felt his chest begin to loosen.

She returned shortly with a partially filled out check. She stood at the screen door and looked at Bomanicials. "Who do I make this out to?"

He said, "William James Washington or W. J. Washington will be fine."

"Who is that?" she asked with a puzzled look on her face.

"That is me. That is my name," he replied.

"I thought your name was 'Bomanicials," she said.

"When you ax my name when I started to work for you three years ago, I say my name is 'William James Washington, but can call me by my initials."

The Night Liberace Landed in Lubbock, Texas

"What's in this box, Mama?" I had promised my mother I would help her clean out Daddy's things. It had been over a year since his death, so it was past time. We had already been to the Goodwill store once and the garbage dump twice.

My two older brothers, David and Mark, were allegedly helping. We were fortunate to all live short distances away and could devote an entire weekend to Mama and house cleaning. They were supposed to be going through Daddy's office and his so-called "workshop in the garage." The last time I checked on them my older brother, David laughed and said, "Dad had three of everything and one of them might work." I suspected they were in the garage drinking beer.

As the only girl and the baby, I was assigned to be with Mama for the cleanout of Daddy's things. "In the event she cried" they said. What if I cried?

"I have no idea," Mama said reaching for the dusty shoebox. "I have no idea what is in this box or in this closet. I don't think I have been in here for over 40 years."

We sat together on the closet floor in front of a large brown trunk. Even at almost 75 years old Mama was still spry and flexible and could probably get up from the floor better than I could at almost 45.

I knew my brothers dreaded this as much as I did. We were memories of the only home we had ever known. When Daddy died suddenly, the family dynamics shifted. We were all dealing with memories.

"Oh, my word!" I heard my mother say. It was one of Mother's favorite expressions of surprise. Depending on how she said it, it could signal doom or happiness.

"Oh, my word!" she said again looking at an old newspaper clipping. "This was the night your Daddy proposed to me." Her eyes grew misty, yet they glowed with a warm happiness of a forgotten time.

I took the yellowed newspaper column from her. It was from the Lubbock Morning Avalanche, dated June 9, 1956. The headline in bold read: *Local waitress wins contest to meet famous piano player*. Beneath it was a photograph. "Is that you and Daddy?" I asked. "Who is the piano player?"

"NEVER!" she screamed. "Never call Liberace a piano player!" she cried abruptly. "I could not believe the newspaper called him that. Stupid paper. Lubbock is flatter than a ten-year-old girl. Why name the newspaper after a snowstorm on a mountain? And 'Morning?' as though avalanches are timed. Should have called it The Dust Daily. Liberace was an artist. A musical genius. And yes, that is me and your Daddy."

I quickly reached for my phone to Google 'Liberace.' My mother continued. "Yep, that's me all right. I remember that day like it was yesterday. I was working at the Hi-D-Ho Drive-In on 3rd Street and College in Lubbock." I decided to switch from reading about Liberace and Google the Hi-D-Ho Drive-In.

"Lubbock, Texas was booming back then," she continued. "Cotton prices were sky high. My Daddy bought Mama a 1954 green Ford four-door car and gave me the old 1945 gray Chevy farm truck."

"Most folks don't know about music in Lubbock. There was The Cotton Club and Fair Park Coliseum." I wondered if the people of Lubbock knew about The Cotton Club of Harlem. I doubted it.

"The Hi-D-Ho Drive-In was where all the kids hung out. High school kids and college kids. The specialty was the Hidy Burger. Buddy Holly and the Crickets were in high school. They used to play at the Hi-D-Ho all the time. They played on the roof," she laughed. Now, I was Googling 'Buddy Holly.'

"Elvis Presley even came to town that year. He and Buddy Holly played together at The Fair Coliseum. He came back that October if I recall. Elvis. Not Buddy Holly."

I discovered a photograph of the Hi-De-Ho Drive-in online. "Did you wear an outfit like this?" I asked showing her my phone. Mother laughed. "I sure did. I remember them little red jackets with gold rick rack and matching red pants. Those pants were big and comfy. In the summertime we wore shorts."

"You wore shorts! In 1956? Did you wear roller skates too?"

"Of course, I did. I was good too. I could spin around with my tray over my head and still not spill a drop of a Purple Cow. All of the carhops wore roller skates. I did the first year I worked there. But then I got promoted to indoor supervisor and wore more of a waitress outfit. I still had to wear that stupid hat. I thought the jackets and that flat pill box hat with that elastic band under our chins made us look like bellhops." I didn't know what a bellhop was

54

but decided not to look for the definition at this time. I was still in awe that my Mother knew Buddy Holly.

"Wait!" I looked up. "What is or was a Purple Cow?" I asked.

"Oh it was the rage at the time. I made a many of one. It was grape juice concentrate, milk and ice cream together in a blender."

"I'm sorry, Mama, but that sounds disgusting," I replied trying not to imagine.

"I didn't care for it myself, but all the high school kids seemed to like it. I preferred a cherry lime phosphate. Where was I? Oh yeah. Your Daddy had gotten that football scholarship to Texas Technological College. That is what it was called back then. Now it's Texas Tech University. He wasn't very good, but then again neither was the entire football team."

Harold had graduated that May. We had been dating for almost two years, since I was eighteen and started working at the drive-in. He said as soon as he graduated and found a good job, we would get married."

"Go back to Liberace, Mama. Didn't you like rock and roll?"

"Oh sure, I liked rock and roll, but at 3:30 in the afternoon Liberace would come on the TV set. I would watch it on the old Philco TV in the drive-in. There wasn't no color TV back then, but I could tell Liberace often wore sparkly outfits. He would wear a tuxedo with long tails with a starched shirt and a bow tie. He would walk on to the stage, take a bow, then flip those long tails and sit in front of a baby grand piano. He always had a candelabra on the piano. His voice was soft and smooth. But it was the way he looked at you. Even through the TV screen, it was almost like he knew everything about you. He knew just what you needed to hear to make your day better. And he always made it better by music. There wasn't anything in Lubbock that looked or sounded like Liberace."

"So how did you get to see him?" I asked.

"It was a Sunday morning. I was working at the Hi-D-Ho and business was slow. Being that most everybody was in church, you know. There was two cowboys sitting in a booth reading the AJ. 'Look here,' one of them said. 'Wanda June?' he called out to me. You seen this? Ain't this that fellow you listen to in the afternoon? That fancy dude who plays the piano?'"

I rushed over and grabbed the paper out of his hand. They probably wouldn't have seen the announcement except it was on the same page as the obituaries. Sure enough, right there on page 69. Liberace was coming to Lubbock. The announcement said he was making a personal appearance at the Lubbock Municipal Coliseum on Saturday, June 9, at 8:30 P.M. Tickets were available at the auditorium box office.

All Day Monday, I tried to call the box office to see how much the tickets was. I even remember the phone number – I reckon because I dialed it so many times – PO 2-4616.

I kept trying for about an hour until Howard, the owner of the Hi-D-Ho, made me quit. He said I was tying up the pay phone at the drive-in. Soon as I got off work that day at 5:00, I drove the pick-up down to the coliseum as fast as the old rattle trap would go. Still didn't get there in time. They was already sold out. It didn't matter no how. I couldn't afford $35 a ticket. I cried all the way over to Mr. Martin's record store on Main Street. I remember I was buying your Daddy the new Patsy Cline record he wanted. As I was about to check out, Charlie Johnson from the newspaper walked in and asked Mr. Martin if he could put a poster in the window. It was announcing a contest. It was a chance to win tickets to see Liberace.

I remember it read something like – All ladies in Lubbock and surrounding areas are encouraged to enter. In 100 words or less write an essay called "Why I Want to Meet Mr. Liberace." The winner will receive two front row seats to see Mr. Liberace for her and a guest and get her picture taken with him. The winner will also receive a new dress and a new hairdo compliments of Bertie May's

Dress Shoppe and Beauty Salon on College Street. It went on to say the contest was sponsored by the Lubbock Avalanche, radio station KBVA and TV station KDUB.

"So, you entered and won? How did that come about?" I jumped up and called for my brothers to come inside. I knew they had to hear the rest of this story too.

David and Mark rushed into the room. "What's wrong? Are you all right Mama?"

"Mama got to meet Liberace," I said.

"Who?" They both asked at the same time.

"He was a famous piano... artist and musician," I replied saving myself just in time from mama's wrath. "And she knew Buddy Holly too." I handed them the newspaper clipping.

David asked "Is that Daddy in a suit and a tie? How did you get Daddy wear that?"

"Wait," Mark said. "Buddy Holly? The guy who would have been bigger than Elvis if he hadn't died in that plane crash? That Buddy Holly? Wow!"

"That's the one," Mama replied as a matter of fact. "Very sad day when Buddy and those others died. February 3, 1959, it was. "The music in Lubbock really died that day." We all pondered Buddy' greatness tragically cut short.

I broke the silence and said "Mama entered this contest to meet Liberace and won. She was just about to tell us about her entry. Go on, Mama."

We sought out chairs and settled in to hear Mama's story.

"As I was telling, I was there when Mr. Johnson from the Avalanche put up the poster about the contest in Mr. Martin's record store. In 100 words or less you had to tell why you wanted to meet Mr. Liberace."

"Do you remember what you wrote, Mom? Mark asked.

"Of course, I do," she said." It was something like this."

'Dear Mr. Liberace,

I would like to meet you because you are nothing like anything in Lubbock. Every afternoon at 3:30, I watch your program on KDUB.'

"I thought it would be a good idea to mention the radio

station seeing that they would be judging the entries," Mother said.

You are the best part of my day. I am a waitress at the Hi-D-Ho Drive-in.'

"I thought it would be a good idea to mention the drive-in

too."

'"You always know how to make the world bright with your music and your smile. When you sing your theme song, I pretend you are seeing me through the TV and singing only to me. Meeting you would be the thrill of my lifetime.

Yours truly, Wanda June Jackson

I began to Google Liberace's theme song.

"I don't know how many entries they got, but I guess there

was a judging of some sort. Anyways, the top ten entries were

published in the Sunday Avalanche. I made the top ten. Then folks was asked to vote by calling in to the radio station KBVA and voting for their favorite. You could vote as many times as you wanted to."

"Howard was so happy I mentioned the Hi-D-Ho, he made everybody who came in the drive-in call and vote for me. He even gave them the dime to call.

Then a few days before the concert the radio announced there were two finalists and the TV station was going to surprise the winner and she would be on the 5:00 news. It was like the Miss American Contest. You know if the winner was not able to attend, the runner-up could go.

"Who was the other contestant, Mama? Did you know her?" I asked.

Mama thought a moment and said "I think it was a girl from Idalou. Don't recall her name. Maybe her name was Idalou, and she was from Shallowater. I forget."

"But I knew I had won when I saw the T.V. truck pull up in front of the drive-in. I ran in the back and put on some lipstick and ran a comb through my hair. When I came out, Howard was greeting them. I just stood there grinning like a raccoon while Joe Bob Allen announced me as the winner.

Mark said shook his head and said, "I can't believe you not only got Daddy to go with you, but he wore a suit and tie."

Mama sighed and said "Well actually, when Lynn Davis from Davis' Menswear heard that Bertie May was donating a dress and a hair do, he wanted to donate some clothes too to get his name mentioned in the program. Mr. Davis was so cheap your Daddy had to return the clothes the next day. Reverend Miller at the Baptist Church bought the suit. Every time we'd see him at church wearing it your Daddy and I would laugh. I got to keep my dress though."

David asked, "How did you and Daddy get there?"

"A limousine picked us up at the Hi-D-Ho and took us to the coliseum. We'd never seen a limousine before let alone ridden in one. I felt like a movie star. When we got to the coliseum there was a man in a fancy suit that opened the door and helped me out. Then me and your Daddy were escorted to the front row seats. I was so excited I almost peed in my pants.

The lights dimmed and when Mr. Liberace came out on the stage, I almost fainted. I swear he winked at me. He played almost an hour and a half. He played all kinds of music. Then he stood up and took a bow and said, 'Now before I play my last number, I want you to meet the little lady who won the Meet Liberace contest.' He motioned for me to come up on stage. He said 'Come up here, Miss Jackson. You too, sir,' motioning for Harold. Your Daddy didn't want to go, but he did anyway. My knees were shaking so hard I was afraid you could see them knocking together. I was scared I was going to trip and fall going up to the stage.

He said, 'This is Miss Wanda June Jackson.' Everybody clapped. Liberace kissed me on the cheek and shook hands with Daddy. He thanked me for coming. The newspaper took our picture we sat back down. Then Liberace dedicated his theme song to me! To little old me! I thought I was going to die right then and there."

I remembered I was Googling 'Liberace theme song.'

Mama continued. "Then it was over and time to leave. The T.V. station could only afford the limousine one way, so we had taken your Daddy's truck down earlier so we would have a ride home."

"Wow, Mom!" Mark said, "That is a great story."

"And that was the night Daddy proposed to her," I said.

"Really?!" The boys cried together.

"Yep. It was after 11:00 and drive-in was closed, and Harold pulled around to the back," Mother said.

"The drive-in was closed at 11:00?" David asked.

Mama gave him a puzzled look and said, "It was Lubbock!" she said emphatically. "There is not much to do there in the daylight, let alone when it's dark," she laughed. "The sidewalks rolled up after dark. Besides, church was the next day."

"Go on, Mom. What happened next?" Mark asked.

"Well, your Daddy had talked Howard into giving' him a key to the drive-in. It was just the two of us. I didn't know what was fixing to happen. The only light was coming from the juke box.

He took my hand and we walked over to the juke box. He said "Some new records came in today. Ain't been played yet." He reached in his pocket and pulled out a nickel, put it in the coin slot and pressed the buttons. Your Daddy sure could dance."

Mark said "Yes, he could. I am glad he taught me to dance."

"Me too," said David.

"I loved to dance with Daddy. Do you remember the song?" I asked.

"Of course. It was *Modern Don Juan*. One of Buddy Holly's first hits. He was getting pretty well-known by then.

David said, "I found it." He pressed play on his phone.

Well, I ain't nothing but a man in love;
I ain't nothing but a man in love
The girls that say I'm the only one.
They even say I'm a Modern Don Juan

David stood and grabbed Mother from the chair, and they began to two-step around the room.

"Ooh, I love her so; I'm never ever going let her go..."

"Mother! You are going to break a hip!" I laughed. Mark stood and we joined in, each of us taking turns dancing with Mother. We laughed so much we were all crying.

"That is so cool, Mama," Mark said as we sat down.

Her eyes became misty, and she said, "Then he put another nickel in the juke box, and pressed E 17. He got down on one knee and said, 'Wanda June, I got the job in Dallas. Will you marry me?'"

Then Liberace's theme song begin to play," she said. Tears began to swell in Mother's eyes.

I looked at my phone to see 'Liberace's theme song – *I'll Be Seeing You* was ready. I pressed play on my phone, and we heard the opening strains.

I'll be seeing you in all the old familiar places; that this heart of mine embraces all day through.

My brother David stood and asked mother to dance.

'In that small café; the park across the way; the children's carousel; the chestnut tree; the wishing well..."

Then Mark and I joined in with them.

I'll be seeing you in every lovely summer's day; I'll be seeing you in everything that's light and gay; I'll always think of you that way. I'll find you in the morning sun, and when the night is new. I'll be looking at the moon, but I'll be seeing you."

We continued to stay entwined, embracing each other long after the song ended. We dried our tears and hugged. We eased back into our chairs.

Mama sighed and said "So we got married that August and moved to Dallas. I guess you know how that story ended."

"What an amazing story," David said.

Mark seconded it with "It sure is. We never knew you were famous."

She laughed "Well, it didn't take too much to make almost anybody famous in Lubbock, Texas."

I looked at the newspaper clipping. June 5, 1956. I looked at my brother David and asked, "David, when is your birthday?"

"February 9, 1957. Why?"

Mama grinned and said, "And that's how I got your Daddy to wear a suit and tie the night Liberace landed in Lubbock."

Mary LoRaine Burns

In 1976 every small town in America had a Bicentennial Celebration that included a parade. Sarasota, Texas was no exception. It was a good thing the fire truck was going by when the Statue of Liberty caught on fire. Otherwise, the whole neighborhood could have gone up in smoke. That was the good news. The bad news was that all five of the lawn judges were riding on the fire truck. The even worse news was that Clark Carter, the editor of the Sarasota Examiner was riding on board the fire truck with his camera and took pictures of the entire incident.

Let me back up. Nobody in the family could exactly pinpoint the day Mary LoRaine went crazy. She came out of me crazy and always was just a little crazy growing up. She refused to be called 'Mary' in elementary school because there were two other Marys in her grade. I could understand that, but she wanted to be called

'Gloria' and that was not her name. She was named after my grandmother Lois and Harold's grandmother Raine. I told her it was either going to be Mary or LoRaine, but it was not going to be Gloria or Fanny or any other name that was not on her birth certificate. Harold and I often wondered if there had been a mix up at the hospital when she was born.

She'd grown up always thinking up crazy things. Things that were going to make her rich and famous. When she was 13, she was going to be a model and didn't eat anything for a week except celery and cabbage. When she was 16, she decided to become a poet and refused to leave her bedroom until she had written a book of poetry. She stayed there for two weeks until the swimming pool opened, and I told her she could go to the pool by herself.

After high school, she went to that school in Kilgore and became part of that Rangerette dancing team. She made an A in dance and either a D or an F in just about everything else. But she did meet and marry Dennis Burns, so it was not a total waste of money.

The first Christmas after she and Dennis bought a home on Washington Avenue, she lined the driveway with all blue Christmas lights. It looked like an airport runway waiting for an airplane to land. Harold said he had several complaints at the Western Auto Store we owned in town. People complained that the strings of lights sold at the store did not have any blue lights. When neighbors drove by LoRaine's house at night they realized why.

Then one time she decided to make holiday hats. She showed up for the candlelight Christmas Eve service wearing a large Christmas present wrapped in silver wrapping paper with a bright red bow on her head.

Overall, most of her crazy schemes were harmless and nobody took notice, at least until she got older. Her husband Dennis said it could have been after both children were grown and had gone. Dr. Thompson said it could have been the change of life. As her mother, I thought it could have been either or both of those, but mostly because she was the middle child and only girl of three. Those children are more prone to craziness. Nevertheless, it was the summer of 1976 that the entire town of Sarasota knew LoRaine was bat-crap crazy.

Just adding another crazy person to Sarasota wasn't anything new. We have had lots of crazy people over the years. There was that widow Ware who lived on Fourth Street. She fell in love with Jeb Stuart. Nothing wrong with falling love, mind you, but Jeb Stuart had been dead 112 years, having died during the War Between the States in 1864. As if that were not enough to make you wonder where her senses went, she planted her entire front yard in the shape and colors of the Confederate stars and bars.

Then there was Billy Carr. He did something for the school district, but no one was exactly sure what his job was there. He mostly just walked around town on the weekends saying "Hello" to everybody he saw. That was all that Billy really knew how to do.

None of the town's crazy people posed any danger or threat to anybody. Mary LoRaine certainly didn't. At least not until she almost burned down the whole town.

You know the phrase, 'Champagne taste on a beer budget?' LoRaine was a beer budget with no taste. This was most evident if one ever went to her house. The living room sofa was a bright orange something called "Naugahyde." What in the Sam Hill was Naugahyde? Were naugas some little, exotic animals who give their hides to become someone's couch? I think it was some kind of fake leather. LoRaine said it was all the rage and made Dennis work overtime at the Western Auto so she could buy one. Whatever it was, it was uncomfortable, as well as ugly. When you sat on it, the cushion made a kind of whooshing and hissing sound as air squeezed out.

Then there was that avocado green chair that LoRaine said was a perfect match. It really wasn't the color of an avocado. It was more like the green of a rancid olive. It too was fake upholstery. Those two pieces of fruit-colored furniture along with Dennis' sensible, brown fabric recliner all sat on lime green shag carpet. It looked like a polyester sheep gave its coat to be dyed green to make it. I supposed it matched if you were enrolled in a School for the Blind.

Anyway, it all seemed to start back in June of 1976. I stopped by LoRaine's one morning on the way to Peterson's Drug Store to see if she needed anything. When I walked in the living room, the big picture books that sat on the coffee table were moved and stacked to the side of the room by the orange Naugahyde sofa. On the coffee table sat eight rolls of beige freezer tape, a pair of scissors, a couple of bottles of rubber cement, a small can of clear shellac and two sets of men's underwear in the form of white T-shirts and white boxer shorts.

LoRaine was sitting on the floor surrounded by magazines, notebooks and papers and pencils of all different colors. "LoRaine? What in tarnation are you up to now?" I asked.

"Mama!" she exclaimed. "I am going to be a fashion designer. Look I already thought up some business cards. "Which one of these do you like best?" She handed me two index cards. The first one read, *"LoRaine Burns Gowns."*

I frowned while I weighed the discomfort of joining her on the floor or having body parts stick to the hissing Naugahyde sofa. I went with the sofa. I looked at her and said, "LoRaine? I do not think three years of high school homemaking and looking at pattern books at the J.C. Penny's qualifies you to design night gowns or anything else."

"Oh Mama, don't be silly. Not night gowns. Evening gowns and cocktail dresses. Formal wear," she replied.

"Where in Sarasota does anybody wear evening gowns?" I questioned.

"You do, Mama! You and Sarah and all your friends when you have your Worthy Matrons meetings at the Eastern Star," LoRaine said.

"We do have to wear a fancy evening dress, but we only do that one time a year, so we wear the same dress every year. Those old women can't remember what they wore yesterday, let alone over a year ago."

I looked at the second index card and asked, "LoRaine have you read this?"

"Of course. Why?"

"Well it says, *Designs by LoRaine. Expert Sewer.* S-E-W-E-R. Maybe you should have gone with seamstress. This sounds like you are designing something for when the septic tank overflows or the toilet backs up."

She angrily grabbed the cards from my hand and angrily tore them into pieces. "I will work on the business card design later."

"LoRaine, I am not certain about this. This is just another one of your crazy ideas. It is just like the time I said you could cater my Daughters of the Texas Revolution meeting It will be as embarrassing as that was."

"How was I supposed to know that it is against the law to pick bluebonnets in Texas?" she huffed.

"LoRaine," I said trying not to raise my voice over dead bluebonnets. "It is not against the law to pick the state flower of Texas. It is against the law when there is a No Trespassing sign on the fence! Besides, I am not talking about the flower picking. I am talking about the punch!"

LoRaine got up from the floor, took a seat in the avocado and lit a cigarette. She blew out a stream of blue smoke and said, "Well, how was I supposed to know the ice in the punch bowl would melt so fast. I had a color scheme. The punch was red; the ice ring was white; and the flowers frozen in the ice ring were blue. The ice just melted too fast."

"Melted it did! You sat the punch bowl in front of the window unit and the air conditioner blew directly **on** the punch bowl. By the time the refreshments were served I had a sopping mess of wet blue bonnets floating in my grandmother's crystal punch bowl. Patty Harris and Thelma Steen laughed so hard that Patty had an asthma attack and Thelma peed in her pants on my kitchen floor. My whole Sunday school class knew about it the next day."

"Well, the cookies shaped like Texas with a raisin marking where Sarasota is turned out good." LoRaine responded in defense.

I pointed to the stuff on the coffee table and asked, "What is all of this mess? What are you going to make your dresses out of? Freezer tape and shellac?"

"If I am going to design and make dresses, I need a dress form. I figure half of the women in town are your size and the other half are about my size. We are going to make some dress forms. I can fit my dresses on the form before the ladies come over for their fittings."

This was not sounding good, but I asked anyway. "So, you want to make a dress form that is chubby and enjoys good food and one that is a beanpole skinny malnourished looking like you?"

"I am not malnourished!" LoRaine cried. "I'll have you know I can still fit into my twirler uniform from when I was in high school."

I ignored the false rationale and bit my tongue struggling not to say that I was thinking, *I could fit into almost anything I wore in high school if I had enough fabric to alter it.*

"See Mama? You take off your clothes down to your panties and brassier and put on Dennis' T-shirt. Then you put on his boxer shorts over your panties. I will wrap the tape around you and use the rubber cement to help hold it together. Then I will put a coat of shellac over it to seal it. After it all dries, I will cut it up the back, tape it back together and it will be in the shape of your body."

"Let me see if I understand this right. You want me to go in the bathroom, get almost necked, put on my son-in-law's underwear, and then let you strap me up like a mummy from Egypt? This is the worst idea ever to come out of your brain. I think it is all them fumes from the hair spray making your brain like an egg in the frying pan. This is your brain on drugs. This is your brain on hair spray. No way. Absolutely not. I am not going to let you shellac me in freezer tape. You can get your friend Earlene to wrap you up like a sausage, but I am going to the drug store."

It was early morning two days later when I was on my way to the Piggly Wiggly for groceries, that I drove by LoRaine's house and saw it. I pulled into her driveway, got out and knocked on the door. LoRaine was in her bathroom and still had hot rollers in her hair when she opened the door. "I see Earlene must have let you tape her up," I said.

"Well, Good Morning to you too, Mama. Why are you here? Is something wrong? It is Daddy? Or Dennis?" she asked as I slid passed her.

"Yes, Earlene and I did make a dress form, but when I was putting on the shellac the fumes made us both dizzy. Earlene fell on the sofa. I fell on top of her. Our falls tore out the left arm hole, so we threw it away. Why are you asking?"

"LoRaine! Dogs got into your garbage can and that dress form thing you tried to make is in Mrs. Pettijohn's azalea bushes. It looks like a naked, decapitated, armless, legless body is lying there. You know how Myrtle Pettijohn is about her azaleas and her flowers. You just better hope she hasn't seen it and called the sheriff."

LoRaine stormed out the front door, hot rollers and all and stomped next door into Mrs. Pettijohn's yard. She retrieved the torso and tossed it into the garbage can in the garage. That should have been the end of that.

The Bicentennial of July 4, 1976, fell on a Sunday. Our parade was Saturday, July 3. I usually helped out Harold and Dennis at the Western Auto store on Saturdays anyway. Harold had owned the Western Auto Store since we were married almost 50 years ago.

With the parade being that day and the route going right in front of the store, we knew it was going to be extra busy. LoRaine had of course entered the Chamber of Commerce's yard decoration contest and stayed in front of her house. She said she would join us as soon as the fire truck with the judges went by.

I was happy that LoRaine did not go overboard with her yard decorations. She and Earlene built a papier-mâché statue of The Statue of Liberty. It sat at the end of the sidewalk in front of LoRaine and Dennis' house. Even though it was life size, it was a simple decoration.

It was hot and steamy that day and simply perfect for a Fourth of July parade. The parade was to start up at the high school and proceed down Washington Avenue to the railroad tracks. At that point vehicles and floats would turn left, while horses and wagons turned right. This was to help clear traffic after the parade.

As expected, the day of the parade the route of the parade was crowded. People lined both sides Washington Avenue. The lines stretched along the two-mile march from the high school to the railroad tracks. It seems everybody in the county and the surrounding ones came to town. Harold stepped outside the store about 10:00 that morning to see if the parade had started. He returned to let everybody know that he heard the Sarasota High School band playing so it would not be long before the parade was in front of the store. The few customers, Dennis, and I stepped outside while Harold locked the door.

The Sarasota High School Marching Band marched down the street in front of us. Then the Mayor Sam Gibson and Sheriff Johnny Watson rode by in convertibles. Then there was a long gap where nothing was coming down the street. That was when we saw the smoke and heard the sirens. Sheriff Watson's car made a U-turn and raced toward the towering smoke.

Nobody knew what happened until Gary Hawkins came down the street and announced the cause. "There was a crazy woman in a twirling outfit twirling a fire baton to Stars and Stripes Forever in her front yard. Both flaming ends flew off. One landed in some lady's flowers and the other one caught this Statue of Liberty decoration on fire. They stamped out the fire in the lady's yard right quick. But the statue had some kind of flammable stuff on it. This is why it caught fire so fast. Nobody got hurt and the fire didn't spread. Good thing the fire truck was right there."

Harold, Dennis, and I looked at each other. Harold and Dennis had that well-we-have-to-work look, so I knew I was the designated responder. Harold reopened the stored. I grabbed my purse and drove to LoRaine's. The Sarasota fire truck was still there, but the Anderson-Shiro Volunteer Fire Department was hauling off the charred remains of Lady Liberty.

LoRaine said, "Come in" when I knocked on the door. She was still in her twirling outfit sitting on the orange Naugahyde and smoking a cigarette. Ignoring the irony, I asked "Are you all right? I am so sorry."

"No! I am not all right. I singed all of the hair off my arms and became the laughingstock of the town. Clark will have it on the front page of tomorrow's paper."

I tried to think of something comforting, but she was probably right about Clark. I said, "Dennis said, since you weren't hurt, he would come by and check on you at lunch. What went wrong – aside from the fact that you have not twirled a fire baton since high school? Where did you even find one?"

"I didn't. I made one." LoRaine replied blowing a stream of blue smoke.

Afraid to do so, but I asked anyway. "You made a fire baton? How?"

"I wired some Kotex pads to the ends of one of my old batons."

"And...?"

"I soaked them in kerosene all night. As soon as lit them and started to twirl one of the Kotex flew off into Mrs. Pettijohn's front yard. The other flew into Lady Liberty's torch. But I swear there was not even enough flame left to start that big of a fire. Suddenly, the whole thing was on fire. Just like that. Whoosh."

I don't know what made me ask, but I did. "LoRaine? What happened to that dress form you tried to make?"

"Earlene and I used it to make the Statue of Liberty. Why do you ask?"

"Didn't you coat the freezer tape with shellac?"

"Yes and used the rest of it to seal the Statue of Liberty." I sighed and asked, "LoRaine, you do know that shellac is flammable? It's a wonder you didn't catch fire."

"Well then, it was Dennis' fault."

"Why is it Dennis' fault?" I asked in shock.

"He brought me the supplies from the store."

I looked up and said, "Here comes Dennis now."

Dennis walked through the back door and into the living room. Before he could say anything, LoRaine lit into him. "Why did you sell me flammable shellac?"

He just looked at her and calmly replied "All shellac is flammable, LoRaine." The man is a saint or should be after being married to my daughter.

"I came to tell you that Sheriff Watson is on his way. In fact, there he is now." Dennis said looking out the front window. LoRaine jumped up and ran into the bedroom slamming the door.

Dennis opened the front door and invited Johnny Watson inside. "Howdy, Dennis," he said. "Hello, Mrs. House," he said addressing me before turning his attention back to Dennis. "I am so glad nothing serious happened today, but I still need to talk to LoRaine. Is she here?"

Just then LoRaine burst back into the room like Loretta Young at a cotillion. She had done a quick change into a red, white, and blue sun dress, reapplied make-up and redone her hair. AquaNet fumes preceded her into the room.

"Hello Sheriff," she gushed. "I am so sorry about this morning. Dennis did not tell me shellac was flammable."

Johnny shot Dennis a pitiful look. Dennis just shrugged.

"Well, LoRaine, given that nothing was seriously damaged, and nobody got hurt, you probably saved yourself from going to jail. But I still must issue these citations and you have fines to pay."

"Fines!" LoRaine screamed. "Like what?"

"Well, there are property damages for $100," he stated as a matter of fact.

"What property?" It was my property!" she continued in disbelief.

"Mrs. Pettijohn's," he replied, "for when the bystanders stomped out the fire in her flower bed destroying one of her azalea bushes and a row of her pansies and petunias."

"That is outrageous. Pansies and petunias do not cost $100," LoRaine cried.

Sheriff Watson replied, "It also includes Mrs. Pettijohn's mental anguish for seeing her flowers stomped."

"Mrs. Pettijohn does not have enough mental capacities to anguish seeing her flower stomped on," LoRaine huffed.

Johnny continued "Then there are two county fire code ordinances for $100 each and one city ordinance for $100 for a fire in the city limits. I think that totals $300. You will have to go the courthouse in Anderson to pay."

Before LoRaine could react, Dennis reached and took the papers from Johnny's hands. Sheriff Watson said, "Thank you, Dennis. See you at the Lion's Club meeting on Monday." Dennis followed him out and returned to the Western Auto. He was probably calculating how much overtime would be needed to pay LoRaine's fines.

LoRaine was still mad and now added pouting to her mood, so I said I was leaving too. Just as I was walking out the door, Clark Carter pulled into the driveway. Clark had gone to high school with LoRaine's older brother Bill. Bill always said Clark had a crush on

LoRaine, but she hardly gave him the time of day. Bill would later

say that Clark dodged a bullet.

"Well crap! Now what does that little squirrel bait want?"

LoRaine cried. I sat back down on the Naugahyde ignoring the

wheezing whoosh.

Before Clark could ring the doorbell, LoRaine yanked the

door open and said "I suppose you want an interview. Well, I am not

going to give you one. No comment, There!"

Clark laughed and came inside.

"Hello, Mrs. House. It is good to see you." Turning to LoRaine

he said, "An interview would be great, but that is not why I am here.

I can piece the story together myself. I was sitting on the fire truck

and saw the whole thing. Remember?" He took a seat next to me on

the Naugahyde Orange.

"Don't sit down," LoRaine said.

Clark ignored her and said, "LoRaine, I got some really good photographs this morning. I got this new camera at The Examiner. It just came out and is called a Canon AE-1. The AE stand for Auto Exposure. It is the first camera to have a microprocessor. I also got this motorized film winder so I can take photographs real fast. Then we also got this machine that lets you send pictures to another news agency..."

"Shut up, Clark!" LoRaine interrupted. "I do not care about your gadgets. I don't even know what a micro do ditty thing is. Now get out."

Ignoring her he continued, "LoRaine, I took an entire roll, or 36 exposure film and I got a couple of really good ones. I developed and printed this one. Do you want to see it? I was taking photographs so fast I got the Stature of Liberty just as the flame hit the torch of the statue. It looks like the statue is holding a real flame. Then there you are standing beside it."

LoRaine looked at the photo and began to smile. Clark went on "With this new machine I was telling you about, I want to send the picture to my fraternity brother from TCU. He works for the Texas Press Association. He has been wanting me to enter something in one of their photography contests, so I am going to enter this one. I need you to sign this consent form because you are in the picture in case, I win a prize."

LoRaine's face lit up when she heard the word prize.

"There is a prize involved?" she asked snatching the paper and pen from Clark and scribbling her name.

"Well, The Examiner would get the prize, but you would still be in the photograph and the prize would hang in the office of The Examiner. Thank you, LoRaine." He stood to leave.

Suddenly LoRaine was all gushy and asked, "So will this be the picture on the front page tomorrow?"

Clark grinned and said, "Unless something else happens before we print the paper."

It was almost 2:00 before I got back to the Western Auto. It was one of the busiest days we ever had except Christmas Eve. We sold out of fire extinguishers and smoke alarms. Dennis made a quick run to Anderson to get some more, and I placed orders for seven people for delivery next week. Everybody was in good spirits and thought the whole incident was funny.

Of course, LoRaine had been born without a sense of humor and saw nothing humorous about it. She refused to come out of the house and come to the store to help us. She wouldn't go the VFW Dance that night with us either. Dennis was so happy he could play pool all night without interruption. He was one of the last to leave the VFW Hall.

Sure enough, Clark put the picture of LoRaine and the flying flaming Kotex just as it ignited the torch on the State of Liberty on the front page of the Sunday Sarasota Examiner. The headline was "LoRaine Burns with Patriotism." The caption beneath read "LoRaine Burns does a fire baton routine as part of her burning patriotism celebrating our country's Bicentennial."

LoRaine was so thrilled about her picture in the paper, she beat me and Harold to church Sunday morning. When Brother Williamson congratulated her over her picture in the paper during the announcements, I had to stop her from standing up and taking a bow.

Of course, she had not bothered to read the entire article. It went on to praise the Sarasota Fire Department for their quick response. They were, after all, sitting right there when the fire broke out. It also listed the winners of the Bicentennial Yard Decoration Contest. Had LoRaine read the column she would not have been happy to see Dorothy Harvey winning first place for her flag display and Beth Bogan winning second for dressing like Betsy Ross sewing the flag with her husband, dressed as George Washington, and holding his hunting rifle.

Seven entries received Honorable Mention. She would have been equally unhappy to see that the column said, "LoRaine Burns' entry was disqualified when it caught on fire."

That fall, the city council passed an ordinance stating that "No holiday decorations were to use flammable substances or use actual fire." This put a damper on LoRaine's Halloween pumpkin porch display.

Also that fall, Clark and The Examiner won second place in the Texas Press Association photography contest. His friend said he would have won first except that photographer in Wichita Falls took a picture of a cow being sucked up by a tornado. The cow lived but wasn't ever quite right afterward. The Examiner got a plaque and Clark's picture of LoRaine and her burning patriotism hung in the lobby of The Examiner.

LoRaine relished in the spotlight for about two weeks that summer and everybody forgot about it until Easter.

That Good Friday, LoRaine's yard decoration was a six-foot, almost full-size scale replica of The Crucifixion scene, complete with mannequins attached. Sheriff Watson and Clark were on their way even before the scene distracted Charlie Tergerson so that he lost control of his pickup truck and ran into it causing one of the crosses to block the street. Another cross mannequin fell across the hood of his truck, crashed through the windshield, and sat in the passenger seat.

Mr. Tergerson was not injured, but EMS was called for his blood pressure. The Sheriff told LoRaine to take it down or get fined for causing traffic issues. He told her she could leave one cross, but no mannequin hanging on it.

This prompted an emergency city council meeting the following week to pass an ordinance against "using seemingly life-size human-looking items in yard decorations."

Clark won first place in the Texas Press Photography Contest that fall for his photo of "Jesus Saves Man in Accident."

LoRaine continued to decorate the front yard for every holiday you could imagine from Sarasota's Homecoming Football Game to Robert Feyman's son's bar mitzvah. She even had a little sign in the front yard that read "LoRaine Burns Yards."

Word spread of LoRaine Burns Yards and people would drive by to see what she had created in her front yard. People began to look forward to seeing the changes.

Other people in town liked her yard so much they began to decorate theirs. Of course, Harold and Dennis loved that since it increased sales at the Western Auto. Dennis put a sign over the counter reminding people that shellacs and other varnishes were flammable.

Me, Harold, and Dennis agreed on one thing about LoRaine. We all learned it a long time ago about families. Families everywhere have a crazy relative. What do you do with them? Sometimes you just got to love them as they are. And sometimes you have to love them from afar.

Good Health to All from Hilley's Rexall

My name is Carl Hilley of the old Hilley's Drugs and Pharmacy. Hilley's Rexall Drug Store and Pharmacy stood at 302 Main Street in Mount Pleasant, Texas. It sat between the Ben Franklin Five and Dime store at 304 Main and the Western Auto Store on the corner of Main and Cherry Street. My grandfather, Clayton Hilley bought the store after he returned from World War I in 1920. He had been a medic in the Army, and it was a good fit.

My father, Sam Hilley, took over shortly after I was born in 1949. My grandfather semi-retired from the store, and he and Grandma Faye bought a camper and traveled. That was when Hilley's became a pharmacy and a drugstore. My father was one of the first graduates from the new University of Houston Pharmacy School. This meant that he could mix prescriptions, combine liquids for elixirs and assemble other medicines prescribed by doctors. Drug stores could only sell over-the-counter type items like Bayer aspirin and Vick's Vapor Rub and various other health related needs such as

Epson salts, hot water bottles, Ben Gay and various bandages and wraps for sprains. Toward the back, one could even find horse and cow medicines and other veterinary supplies.

I read about the change from a drug store to pharmacy in a scrapbook at my grandmother Hilley's house. There were pictures of my grandfather, Clayton, and my grandmother, Faye, and my father and my mother, Clare, standing in front of a giant sheet cake with Hilley's Rexall Drug AND Pharmacy written in blue icing on top of an orange band of icing. It matched the new sign.

It was a big celebration that made the front page of the Mount Pleasant Tribune. There were pictures of the orange and blue Rexall Drug neon sign being changed from Hilley's Rexall Drug Store to Hilley's Rexall Pharmacy and Drug Store.

The store was a long rectangle. If one walked through the clear, glass door a bell suspended on a piece of red yarn rang with a pleasant jingle-a-ling to announce your entrance. To the left was the lunch counter. The counter was long with ten round stools with bright red plastic seats. All but one of the stools had gray duct tape patches where rear ends with keys and purses and jeans with rivets had ripped the plastic over the years.

The countertop was a pale sea-foam green Formica. Ten spots in front of the stools were worn white where beige Melmac plates, cups and saucers carried countless burgers and shakes and cups of coffee to hungry customers over the years.

Monday through Friday and sometimes on Saturday, a seat on one of the stools during lunch time was a treasure. Everybody in town knew that Miss Lucille Harris made the best hamburger in town. The best BLT or grilled cheese sandwiches too. And people ordered her special chicken salad for parties. She would always slide the plate to you and say, "Here you go. Made with love."

If you came in the front door and turned to the right, it would take you alongside the gift area. That side of the store was lined with three six-foot-long by three-foot tall glass cases that housed various items. The wall behind the counter held shelves that showed other gift items not in the glass cases.

Eva Beth Ives had worked the gift counter as a teenager when my grandfather owned the store. She still worked there but now as Eva Beth Morgan. She could almost keep an inventory of items in her head.

Eva Beth, now widowed, was also in charge of the two nearly full-length picture windows that graced either side of the front door. There was always a holiday display in one window and a "What's New at the Store" in the other.

The middle aisle that divided the lunch counter and the gift area was made up of three back-to-back shelves, each six-foot-long and with three shelves top to bottom that held just about anything you wanted. If it wasn't there and Sam Hilley could not find it and

Eva Beth had never heard of it, then a special order was placed for the customer.

In the back was the pharmacy, the counter stood about three-and-a-half-feet high and nine-feet long with a three-foot area dividing where transactions were made. The actual pharmacy was behind the counter and was elevated and walled off, save for long horizontal window. My father enjoyed the fact that from his elevated position he could watch over the store. He enjoyed that people could see him working behind the counter and in the pharmacy mixing elixirs and pouring liquids into large brown bottles, filling prescriptions, and measuring out pills and capsules into little white cylinders with white pop-off tops. He meticulously typed medical labels on an old black Royal typewriter. He would check and double check to ensure the dosage was correct and the customer information was correct. Every customer left with their merchandise and my father smiling and saying, "Good health to all, from Hilley's Rexall."

The store was open Monday through Friday from 7:00 AM to 6:00 PM, and from 8:00 AM to 5:00 PM on Saturday. It was closed on Sunday. Except of course if somebody needed something. Dad did not hesitate to go down in the middle of the night or on Sunday to fill an urgent prescription.

I started working at the family drug store when I was 16 in 1965. My sister and brother worked there on weekends when they turned 16, too. I started as a soda jerk behind the lunch counter. I worked summers and weekends until I graduated from high school and went to college. After I graduated from college, I went to law school. But I always enjoyed working Christmas and spring breaks at the store.

It was on a Christmas break in 1973 that I noticed an auburn-haired girl working behind the counter alongside Miss Lucille. I was working the camera area, taking in film to be mailed off for development and finding the delivered developed pictures. When I took my lunch break, I sat on a stool at the end of the counter near the pharmacy. Miss Lucille winked at me and tossed a burger patty on the old grill. When she sat it in front of me, I asked nonchalantly "Who is that working with you behind the counter?"

Miss Lucille looked over her shoulder and said "Oh she is new. Her family moved here from Dallas last spring. Her daddy is one of the new doctors in town, Dr. Graham. Very nice family – smart, so they say. Her brother is going to that Rice school in Houston and her sister is going to some school in Dallas. She goes to that long-haired-hippie college in Austin. She works here on breaks like you do. Wants to be a doctor like her daddy. Can you imagine a female doctor? A pedestrian that doctors children."

I nonchalantly wiped a grease spot from my chin with a paper napkin. "She got a name?" I asked as I poured ketchup on my French fries. "And the word is pediatrician."

Miss Lucille replied, "Martha Anne. Why you asking?"

"No reason. Just asking," I said, returning to my burger. Miss Lucille raised her eyebrows in mock disbelief and gave me a look as if to say, "like so much thunder."

I finished my burger, which I noticed Miss Lucille conveniently made without my usual onions, I reached in my pocket and pulled out a stick of Double-Mint gum. I unwrapped the gum and put it in my mouth. I then took my ballpoint pen that was clipped on my shirt pocket and printed on the inside of the silver wrapper.

"My name is Carl Hilley. Would you like to go the movies on Saturday?"

I walked to the end of the counter and handed it to her. When she smiled and said yes, I guess we both knew. Two years later, she graduated from college on a Friday, we got married that Saturday, and on Monday she started medical school. She graduated after a few years, went in to practice with her father and soon became the county's favorite pediatrician.

Somewhere and somehow along the way three children were born and our careers prospered. But we still enjoyed working at Hilley's Rexall Drug Store and Pharmacy on weekends and especially during Christmas.

It was a Saturday two weeks before Christmas in 1980. Mom had the kids and Martha Anne, and I were both helping at the store. The store was packed with customers. There had been a cold snap, and it actually felt like Christmas. Christmas music played throughout the store. The smell of kitchen grease and the perfume counter gave the air a heavy sweet smell. Eva Beth had decorated both windows with stencils creating bells and holly leaves and berries in fake spray-on snow. Silver twirling icicles and brightly colored red balls hug from the top of each window. Christmas lights twinkled around the windows' edges. There was Santa Claus and reindeer, candy canes and Christmas trees in the window. The other window displayed the newest Kodak camera, necklaces with matching earrings, perfumes, dusting powders and Christmas specials all creatively placed to attract attention.

The Shepard twins, Sarah and Roma were looking at the Timex watches for their husbands, also twins. Lilly Sanders wanted to buy her granddaughter a Brownie Kodak Camera and there was a line waiting to be checked out at the gift-shop counter.

In the back of the pharmacy, Mrs. Andrews was waiting for a refill of her daughter's cough syrup and Miss Callie Faust was waiting for her tonic. Mr. Faust had been deceased for over 20 years, and somehow his widow became Miss Callie. Every two weeks, without fail, Miss Callie came to town to get her tonic. Miss Callie, at 81 years of age, still drove her car and insisted that her doctor-prescribed tonic was what made her sleep at night. She never missed the nightly two-tablespoon dosage.

Of course, everybody in town and especially Sam Hilley and

Dr. Graham knew it was almost 90 proof alcohol in some nasty-

tasting, vile green liquid. One tablespoon would put a 150-pound

man in a daze and two would completely knock out of 98-pound

little old lady.

The store was so busy that no one noticed when the bell

rang marking the entrance of a well-dressed young Hispanic man.

He removed his hat and walked down the aisle parallel to the lunch

counter and proceeded all the way to the back of the store to the

pharmacy. A few recognized him as the new janitor at the Western

Auto next door. He nodded or smiled at a few customers. He

nodded to Mrs. Andrews and Miss Callie when he reached the

pharmacy.

My dad was working the pharmacy counter. Mrs. Andrews

had just paid for her medicine and Miss Faust was in the process of

getting her green tonic. As they moved away from the counter, the

young man placed a small brown paper sack on the counter. He then removed a blue and gold box of condoms and said, "Too short." My father looked at the man in surprise with widening eyes and said, "Excuse me?"

The man repeated "Too short."

My father began to turn red around the collar. He lowered his voice and said "Sir, these do not come in sizes. There is no small, medium, or large. One size fits all." My father began to look confused.

""No. No. Compré caja ayer. Me voy a casa. Abro y muy corto. Así que traigo de vuelta."

My father looked confused, but tried again, "I am afraid you do not understand. These are made from latex. El Latexo! La Stretchy!"

Now the Hispanic man looked confused. Sadly, my father continued, "Stretch! Stretch out when you, ...uh uh..., when you stretchy out."

Just before the next Christmas carol began in that one second interval of dead silence the man raised his voice slightly and firmly said, "¡No! Usted no entiende. Condón de goma demasiado corto."

The store went silent and, at that moment, the only sound in the store were patties sizzling on the grill and Gene Autry starting to sing Rudolph the Red Nosed Reindeer. And to make it worse, it seemed that everyone, including Martha Anne and I, seemed to want to look at something near the back of the store close to the pharmacy.

Just then my father helplessly called out "Does anyone speak Spanish?"

"I do," said a voice. Not just any voice or anybody. But the Monsignor from St. Joseph's. Following the Monsignor was Sister Mary Kathleen who cheerfully said, "I do too!" as both were coming down the aisle.

The man blushed and said, "No. No. Compré caja ayer. Me voy a casa. Abro y muy corto. Así que traigo de vuelta."

Then Monsignor blushed and said, "He says that he bought the item yesterday and when he got to his house, he realized it was too short."

Just then the man laughed and said "No, no Padre. Abro el paquete y cuento demasiado." Before the Monsignor could translate the man began to count, "Uno, dos, tres, quautro, cinco, seis, siete, oche, nuevo, dias. El cuadro dice DOCE, pero no once, no doce." He raised all ten fingers and said, "solo diez. Dos cortos"

Sister Mary Kathleen cleared her throat and calmly said, "the box only contained ten items, and on the label, it said it contained a dozen. Therefore, it is too short."

My father opened the box to reveal only ten square foil packages. He reached behind him and grabbed another box, quickly put it in the sack with the original box and said, "on the house." The man turned to leave but stopped, turned, and said, "Gracious y Feliz

Navidad, Senor" and calmly walked out of the store with a smile leaving my father in a red-faced stupor. Laughter erupted throughout the store. My father's face turned turnip purple.

Of course, by sundown the entire town had heard the too short story. Initially, my father did not like being the butt of so many jokes. At the First Methodist Church, where we were all members, Brother Edgar said in the announcements the following Sunday that "Our Building Chairman Mr. Sam Hilley, reports that our building fund did not reach its goal of $200. But we did raise $198 – just two short." Snickers and a few outright laughs could be heard.

On Monday morning, Randy Evans stopped by for a cup of coffee and to drop off the doughnuts from the bakery, "Ella May at the bakery sent three dozen, but said she was sorry, because in one box there is only ten." Randy howled with laughter. And the Tail Twister at the Lion's Club told the story amidst knee slapping laugher on Monday night.

Over time, most of the town forgot, except of course at Christmas when suddenly everybody remembered the too short Christmas story. It was told and retold.

It became a running family joke coordinated by my mom. Each Christmas he received at least one present invoking "two short." One year he received a box of a dozen golf balls, but one sleeve was missing two to make the set two short.

One year the entire family gave him a new set of irons and a new golf bag. His excitement faded when Mom said, "There were on sale because the eight and nine irons are missing, so it's two short." Dad was relieved when the two missing irons later surfaced.

My mother bought him a pair of slippers once, purposely in the wrong size. When he tried them on Christmas morning, she said, "They are not too short, are they?"

Over the years Mom, Martha, and I and our three kids always ensured that there was something under the tree that was always too short. He opened T-shirts a size too small, underwear that was too short, various robes that were too short. Eventually, Dad took it good naturedly and would laugh and often ask, "Look at these pants. They are not too short, are they?

Since 1977 we had been hearing rumors of big changes taking place at the corporate offices. Rexall Drugs, Inc. eliminated franchised dealerships and stores. Rexall products were promoted and began to move to larger super drug chains. Family-owned stores were allowed to stay open if were profitable. Fortunately, Hilley's Drug and Pharmacy showed a profit for an extended period of time. But profits began to decline as more and more shopped at Eckerd's. The prices were significantly lower.

Hilley's Drug and Pharmacy closed in 1990.

Dad died at the age of 93. At his funeral, I got up to say a few words. Others had spoken of his achievements, his accomplishments and his goodness and kindness to all people.

I was to give the closing remarks before the closing prayer. I stood behind the pulpit and said, "Dad, you had a good and wonderful life. You made the world a better place for so many people. We love you, and we will all miss you. That is all I have to say. Except for 'Good health to all from Hilley's Rexall.'" I looked up toward the heavens and asked, "Dad, was it too short?" I swear I could hear him laughing as I returned to my seat, along with a snickering congregation.

With All Due Speed

The doors of the police vehicle opened quickly. Two young police officers rushed to the passenger side and opened the backdoor. The three rear-seated passengers exited the car and took their place between the officers.

Mary Alice Hawthorne, the Coldwater Elementary School principal stood between Dr. Charles Kaiser, the Superintendent of Coldwater County Public Schools and Gene Sampson, the Coldwater High School Principal. They represented the administration for the three schools in Coldwater, Alabama – population 350.

The town was small and rural, and a police escort was probably not necessary. But in these troubled times one could not be too careful. Three years earlier, Governor George Wallace stood at the doors of the University of Alabama to keep the university segregated. Even after President Kennedy sent federal troops, the governor refused to budge. Now the public schools were in the firestorm.

Officer Rufus Martin took the arm of Dr. Kaiser while officer Cecil Woods took the arm of Principal Sampson. Mrs. Hawthorne was in the middle. Walking five abreast the officers walked the trio up the sidewalk to the front steps of the high school where the board meeting was taking place.

When they reached the entrance, Rufus looked at Mary Alice and said "I am so sorry, Mrs. Hawthorne that I had to do that. I know it was embarrassing and hurtful to hear all them people yelling such hateful and ugly things – and the town folk we know too! Please know I'm pulling for all three of y'all."

"Thank you, Rufus. It will work out for the best. It always does." Mary Alice smiled back at him. Even when she taught him in the fourth grade so many years ago, he wanted to be a police officer.

Mary Alice had taught almost everybody in Coldwater. The school building was built in 1937 as a public works project during The Great Depression. The old red school bricks were laid by many men in the town who were unemployed, including her father.

Mary Alice was in the 11th grade and one of the first students to attend school in the new building. For good luck, she always touched the gray plaque on the column to the right of the double doors with the WPA notation that read *Built by Works Progress Administration 1937*. She had entered these doors many times over many years as a student, a teacher and a principal. She had never entered under these circumstances, but it was time for a change.

When they reached the front doors, two state officers unlocked them, leaving the local officers outside and allowed the three administrators to enter, and relocked the doors. The two state law enforcement officials and the three educators walked down the narrow hall to the room where the Coldwater County Public School

Board was meeting. The door to the board room held a handwritten sign "Coldwater Public School Board – Executive Session, June 5, 1966."

Mary Alice's fate and the fate of the other two waited on the other side of the closed door. Seven elected officials were sitting behind a table waiting to issue the fates of the three.

"Well," Mary Alice thought, *We made it through the angry, screaming crowd and the hateful racists' signs shoved at us. Whatever happens on the other side of that door we can and will manage.*

Just as the high school principal reached to open the door, Dr. Kaiser stopped him. He looked at Mary Alice and said, "You do not have to do this, Mrs. Hawthorne. The board is going to get rid of me and probably Mr. Sampson, but you do not have to do this. We'll move on. You are two years away from your retirement. Your pension is at stake. Are you sure you want to go through with this?"

Mary Alice looked at him. "Yes," she smiled. "I stand with both of you." She would probably need to move to the city and in with one of her two children. Her husband had left her a little bit of money. Her pension had been for her to travel, not to support herself. She was thankful for that.

"No, Dr. Kaiser and Mr. Sampson," she continued. "I've spent over 40 years teaching the difference between 'principal' as your 'pal' and 'principle' as your 'belief.' Let's go inside."

Joe John Baker and six other white men sat behind the long wooden table. There were several rows of folding chairs available, but all were empty. The group took their seats facing the board. The room was dimly lit, and a wooden speaker's podium stood alone and upright like a statue. As soon as the three were seated, Joe John said "All right, y'all. Let's get started." His voice was strong and purposeful.

It did not surprise Mary Alice that Joe John was in a leadership role. He was a leader when he was in her fifth-grade class.

Joe John Baker took the gavel in his hand and banged it three times to call the executive session to order.

Joe John looked out over the room and over the heads of the three refusing to look them in the eye. "We have two items to consider in executive session. The first is that we are here to learn the decision of the Coldwater County School Board regarding this integration thing." He pulled a single sheet of paper from a manila folder. He put on his reading glasses and began to read.

"It is the unanimous decision of the Coldwater County Public School Board of Trustees that the Negroes of this county will continue to attend schools in the neighboring school district of Holland and will not be allowed to attend school in Coldwater, Alabama."

He removed his glasses and wiped his eyes with his handkerchief. "Before we move on to item two regarding the

125

employment of the school administrators who support the integration of the schools, does anyone have anything to say?"

Dr. Kaiser rose. "May I address the board?" Without waiting for an answer, he stepped to the podium and continued. "It is my duty to remind you that the United States Supreme Court handed down the decision of Brown versus Board of Education in 1954 that declared segregation and 'separate, but equal' schools were unconstitutional and ordered the schools to proceed with all due speed."

"Thank you, Dr. Kaiser," interrupted Baker. "Since the law said, 'with all due speed' it didn't have a firm timeline, we decided we would integrate the schools when we thought it was time," replied Joe John. "We decide what speed was due."

There were a couple of snickers among the board.

Dr. Kaiser continued unmoved, "May I remind you that last year the United States Congress passed a law called The Elementary and Secondary Education Act of 1965? It says the federal government can withhold federal money if the schools do not integrate. That is a great deal of money to lose. I respectfully ask that you rethink your decision. The schools really need that federal money. We could upgrade the school buildings – put a new roof on the elementary school. We could get a library with books and maps at the high school. We could give students and teachers the textbooks and supplies they need."

"So noted," Baker replied as Dr. Kaiser took his seat. "The board is of the opinion that we don't need the federal government telling us what to do and how to educate our kids. Anybody else want to say anything?"

Gene Sampson stood slowly and took a deep breath, "Ah, Hmm." He stuttered and walked to the podium. "J. J.," he began. "I mean Mr. Baker; I have known all y'all since y'all played football for me in high school. I just think you ought to recall that the Booker T. Washington football team has won the state Negro football championship for the past three years. And their basketball team won the past two state championships. Their coach, Willie Williams is good man and a good coach. He raises fine, young men and really, good athletes. And them funds could give us some good lights in the gym and maybe new bleachers and lights on the football field too. Just saying." He took his seat.

Joe John took a deep breath and looked at the others on the board. All but one board member had their heads down refusing to look at the three administrators. Joe John then said, "Moving on to Item Two, the employment of the school administrators that support integration ..."

"Wait, just a minute, Joe John Baker," Mary Alice stood and took a place at the podium. "I did not get my chance to speak, and I plan to speak my piece. I expect all of you to sit up and listen."

There was a certain shuffling of chairs. The board sat straight in their chairs.

"I have known each one of you since you were in diapers. I have taught every one of you in one grade or another in elementary school. Except for you, Daniel. I taught you twice in the second grade. I tutored you after school until you finally learned to read." There was muffled laughter among the board members.

Joe John looked at the other board members and hoped they felt as uncomfortable as he did. He did not like where this was going.

"I am going to ask you to think back to those days when you were students in my classroom. Joe John, do you remember when you and Davis Yarborough, who is sitting right next to you there, were in my third-grade classroom?"

Joe John and Davis exchanged quizzical glances.

"Well, do you? I asked you a question." She said.

"Yes, Ma'am," they whispered in unison.

"I did not hear you. I always taught you to speak up. What did you say?"

Joe John and Davis both swallowed and answered louder, "Yes, Ma'am."

In that moment, a small, gray haired woman wearing wire framed glasses had usurped all the energy and power from the room.

"Do you remember when you two got into a fist fight on the playground?" she asked firmly.

This time the two men just nodded meekly.

"I told both of you if you promised not to fight any more that I would not tell your daddies. Because I knew that you'd both be whipped within an inch of your skinny behinds if your daddies found out. You trusted me."

Joe John and Davis stared at the wooden planks of the floor.

"Cletus Alford. Stand up!" Mary Alice firmly demanded.

Cletus stood up so fast he knocked over his chair.

"Do you remember when you stole fifty cents from my desk when you were in the fourth grade?"

Cletus stood shaking and nodded vigorously.

"You said you just wanted to buy your Mama a Christmas present. I made you clean my classroom every Friday and paid you a dime until you paid back all of the money. You trusted me, didn't you?"

Cletus nodded and sat back down.

"You two - Junior Martin and Billy Ray Henderson?" she said looking at them square in the eye. "Who went down to the Sheriff's office when you mischievous scoundrels were in the sixth grade? Who begged the Sheriff not to punish you severely for putting three raccoons, an armadillo, and a goat in the post office over night?"

The two board members exchanged glances.

"Billy Ray? Who begged your Mama and Daddy to let you stay in school? Would you have gotten that football scholarship to Alabama if it had not been for me and Coach Sampson? No. You would be breaking your back and dying young like your daddy did. You trusted us!"

"And last, You! T. J. Wayne sitting at the end. I reckon you are about the richest man in the county. Maybe the whole state."

T. J. smirked and looked away.

"Wipe that smirk off of your face. I did not like it in the sixth grade, and I don't like it now. Because you certainly do not need to get above your raising with me – or anybody else as far as I'm concerned."

T. J. lit a cigar and blew smoke in her direction.

"It wasn't always like that, now was it?" she questioned him directly. "Your brothers and sister didn't care if they wore blue jeans

132

donated from the church clothing barrels. But you were too embarrassed to come in your old raggedy clothes. You wanted to wear khaki pants like an old man. Who bought you a couple of pair from Sears and Roebuck so you would come to school? You were an old man then and you are an old man now. How you turned out like you did and your brothers and sister turned out so sweet and kind, I will never figure it out. You trusted me not to tell anybody that story and I never did. Until now!"

T. J. angrily smashed his cigar in the ash tray and glared at her.

"In fact, I trusted all of you boys. I thought you trusted me. I watched each of you grow into fine young men, with wives and children that I taught. I taught most of your Mamas and Daddies too! You were men I was proud of. But I am not proud now. In fact, I am ashamed of each and every one of you. I thought I taught you better than this. Coach Sampson taught you better than this."

Mary Alice realized there were tears running down her cheeks.

"This is not about black or white. This is about the education of young people. The education of children – ALL children! I asked you to trust me back then and I am asking you to trust me and Mr. Sampson and Dr. Kaiser now."

She slowly moved away from the podium and returned to her seat.

Dr. Kaiser handed her his handkerchief and Mr. Sampson whispered, "Nice job, Mrs. Hawthorn."

Joe John Baker broke the heavy silence, "The executive session is adjourned. The board meeting is now in recess for 15 minutes."

The state police escorted the three administrators out the back door to avoid the angry crowd outside. Rufus and Cecil were waiting for them to take them to their homes.

It was almost an hour before the crowd outside realized everybody had gone and the building was empty. They had seen the local patrol car leave with Mary Alice and the other two. No one had seen when or where the others went.

Some rumors said most of the board members went to Joe John's fishing camp in northern Alabama. Others said the board members and their families went to see relatives or on vacation. T. J. Wayne was said to have gone to Texas for the remainder of the summer. What the town of Coldwater knew was that they knew nothing.

Then on Sunday a short column called School News appeared below the fold on the Coldwater Tribune.

"At the board meeting last Friday, the Coldwater County Public School Board in a six to one vote decided to allow Negro students to attend the schools in Coldwater if they chose to do so.

The contracts of the elementary and high school principal and the superintendent were renewed for the upcoming school year.

In a statement delivered by telephone, President of the Board, Joe John Baker said "This is not about black or white. This is about the education of young people. The education of children – ALL children."

In other school news it is rumored that new bleachers and new lights will be installed at the football field this fall. The band director said he was exploring costs of new band uniforms."

I Shot the Sheriff

But I Did Not Shoot the Deputy

I took a sip of morning coffee and read the headlines of the local paper,

"Sheriff Ronald "Obie" Cooper dies after illness"

There was a photograph of Cooper with a mustache and cowboy hat looking like Burt Reynolds in *Smokey and the Bandit.* I wondered how old the picture was. He looked about forty. It was probably taken about the time he got the nickname 'Obie.' I scanned the article "... former local Lee County Sheriff, Ronald, 'Obie' Cooper, 86, died of cancer. Survivors include three stepchildren, ...preceded in death by his wife, and numerous other relatives and friends." I assumed the stepchildren belonged to the widow he married. The other two former Mrs. Coopers were not listed.

The obituary went on to state his years of law enforcement service, a number of law enforcement honors and awards, some civic participation, and information about services and memorial donations. It ended with "Any remaining friends are asked to gather at JPST Moose Lodge 684 for dominoes, refreshments and storytelling."

I thought to myself. "There ought to be some doozy stories told." I folded and tucked the paper under my arm and headed out to check on Dad in his assisted-living facility. Since I retired the previous year, my mornings began by sharing the paper with Dad. I could hardly wait to hear what he had to say about this one.

I walked inside Carriage Inn and down the hallway toward my father's room. Each time I swelled with pride at the nameplate on his door.

Dr. Tom Mathews, M.D.

Colonel, USAF (Retired)

World War II Veteran

An American flag was next to the words on the name plate. What was missing was "Fighter pilot, Purple Heart recipient, over 50 missions flown from Corsica." He was interviewed by Joseph Heller for *Catch 22*. Dad received a special invitation from Heller for the movie premier. Dad did not like the book or the movie. He thought it was, in his words, 'stupid.'

I knocked on the door, then opened it and said, "Coffee delivery for Dr. Mathews!" before entering.

I always scolded my sister for taking him for his first Starbucks latte. Now he wanted one every day.

"Come on in. Oh boy, you brought some of that fancy coffee."

Dad, at age 90, was sharp, active, and still full of spit and vinegar. Last year I arranged an hour ride for him in a vintage World

War II bomber. The pilot even let him fly the plane. It probably

added ten years to Dad's life while taking ten years from the pilot's.

I handed him his latte and the newspaper and watched his

reaction. "Ha!" He exclaimed. "I am surprised the old bastard died

of cancer and not a bullet wound from a jealous husband. I told him

for years to quit smoking those Marlboros."

He sipped his coffee and grinned like a naughty choir boy.

I took a seat on the couch, "I understand a bullet wound was

how you got to know Sheriff Cooper in the first place."

"Yep," he laughed. "I have seen more of Sheriff Ronald

Cooper than any man should – even a doctor."

"You and Uncle Frank are said to be the only two who really

know how he got the nickname 'Obie.' Uncle Frank is gone. Now

Obie is gone. I would like to hear the story," I said.

Dad took a long sip and sighed, "Well, your Uncle Frank was

there, and he was actually responsible for the initial actions. But hey, Frank was as good a veterinarian as I was a doctor. And it was his wife."

"You know you are the only one left now. If the weather is pretty, let's go to the story telling at the Moose Lodge. We'll go on the Harley. And before you ask, no, you cannot drive."

Dad shot me a look that said, "You know I could."

Dad and I walked in the lodge shortly after two o'clock. Dad strutted through the doors in his leather jacket with his motorcycle helmet under his arm. He was still such a bad ass.

There were several domino tables with hands shuffling the pieces and two tables with members of the Ladies Auxiliary playing cards. They did not seem to be there to hear any stories. In the back were several tables shoved together with about six old men aged from mid-80's to mid-90's and their middle-aged sons who brought them. We headed toward them.

"Howdy, Tom! Tom Jr." The men greeted us. "We were hoping you would come."

Everybody shook hands. We took a seat and ordered a beer.

Somebody laughed and said, "I reckon this is all of us who are left that really knew Obie. Most folks don't even know his name was Ronald. Somebody start."

Bill Williams began by telling the story about Obie stopping a drunk driver on the interstate.

He asked him where he had been and the fellow said, "To a cock fight across the river."

Obie asked if the guy could show him, and the dumbass jumped in the patrol car and showed him. Obie said the Department of Public Safety was already there, but all that anybody could see or hear were screaming people running through the woods with squawking chickens.

After a round of laughs, Albert Gonzales told the one about the sheriff having to deliver his first baby. It was both his and the sheriff's first baby. He and his wife were speeding to the hospital when Obie stopped them, realized what was happening, delivered the baby, handed it to Albert and promptly fainted. When the ambulance arrived, they just loaded up mother, baby and sheriff and went to the hospital.

For about an hour and a half, stories of the escapades of Ronald "Obie" Cooper rotated around the table. Some recalled stories of kindness and civic duties. Obie never charged the school district to have an officer for extracurricular activities. It saved the school district a significant sum of money. Some stories were sad like the time he had to tell that family that their only child was killed in a car wreck. Walter Shaw said that was the only time he saw Obie cry. Overall, the men agreed that Obie turned out to be a good man and an honest and fair sheriff.

Steve Hinkle said "I hear Ronald was a wild one though in his youth and his early days of being sheriff. Then he up and married that woman with three kids. THREE, mind you!"

As if on cue, all eyes turned toward Dad. He shrugged his shoulders and said "Y'all all know the story. My brother, Frank's wife, Vera, was having an affair with the sheriff. Frank came home one day to find them together. He threatened him with a gun and the gun accidently went off and shot him."

Just then a new round of beers arrived as if to signal for more of the story. Finally, George Mason said, "Come on, Tom. We have heard rumors for years about how suddenly the sheriff was called Obie. It all started after his hospital stay. Rumors also were that you and Frank knew something about it. Tell us!"

Dad grinned and said, "Well, I reckon it won't hurt now. Me and Frank swore we would never tell while Obie was alive. So here goes."

I loved to hear Dad tell stories. It sounded as though he was reading from a book.

"Cooper had just been elected sheriff. He was about forty years old and just as randy as if he was twenty. He was a real lady killer. He had been married twice but was single at the time of the incident. Most of the town knew about his women and escapades. In the spring of 1986, Mrs. Evans, Frank and Vera's next-door neighbor, said something to Frank about seeing the sheriff's car at his house on Wednesdays about noon.

It was just after 1:00 o'clock that Wednesday in April. I had just come back to the practice from lunch at the City Café and was about to start the afternoon appointments. Marlene, y'all remember my nurse, Marlene?"

Heads nodded and a few murmurs of yes could be heard.

"Marlene said Frank was on the phone and said it was an emergency. When I answered, all he said was 'get to my house **now**!'

Before I could ask what was wrong, he hung up. I rushed out with my bag, leaving Marlene to tell everybody I was called to an emergency.

Just as I was turning into Frank's driveway, Vera wheeled out in her Mercedes and almost ran over me. Frank was sitting on the back porch drinking a beer.

'What's wrong?' I asked out of breath.

Frank looked at me and said in a very calm voice, 'I shot the sheriff.'

'You shot the sheriff?'

'Yes. I shot the sheriff, but I did not shoot the deputy,' he laughed.

'Frank,' I said, 'Stop singing Eric Clapton songs. This is not funny. You can go to Huntsville for this.'

'Oh Hell, I just grazed him. If I was going to kill him, I would have. I need you to sew up the wound.'

I was trying to get my head around what had happened. When I asked him why he did not take care of the wound himself if it was minor, he said he had already done his part. I did not know what that meant at the time.

I asked, 'Where is the wound?'

'In his butt,' he said as a matter of fact. Frank stood up and motioned for me to come inside. We walked into the house. He grabbed a bottle of Jack Daniels from the bar.

'It's 1:30 in the afternoon, Frank,' I said. 'What is going on?' We walked down the hallway to the bedroom. As soon as he opened the door, I realized why he picked up the bottle of whiskey. Frank!' I screamed. 'Holy Crap! What have you done?' There was

Sheriff Cooper passed out, naked from the waist down, spread eagle, with hands and legs handcuffed to the bed posts.

'Oh, he's fine,' Frank said calmly. 'I used a mild anesthesia that I use on small animals.'

I could hardly breathe. 'Besides that, what is the towel and all that cotton between his legs?' I reached for the bottle, chugged a big swig and said 'start at the beginning. Start with where's Vera?'

Frank calmly took the bottle and took a swallow. He wiped his mouth on his arm and said 'I told her to get some things, gave her $20 dollars and told her to get out and never come back again. I told her divorce papers would be served as soon as I can get them drawn up. And if she ever showed up or told anybody I would take the other one.'

'The other what?' I asked. He pointed to a Mason jar on the nightstand. 'Oh God. Frank! Hand me the Jack Daniels bottle!'

I had to hold on to the bed post because I was so weak.

'Frank!' I screamed at him 'You castrated the sheriff! Do you know how much trouble you are in?'

Well, we spent the rest of the afternoon trying to figure out our next moves. We drained the bottle of Jack Daniels. While Frank went to the kitchen to fetch another bottle, I stitched up the minor gunshot wound on Cooper's butt."

Dad paused for the effect, took a sip of beer and watched the reaction.

Finally, I stuttered "Uncle Frank castrated the sheriff?"

Joseph Linwood pulled out his inhaler. Cecil McGee spit a mouthful of beer on Robert Doris. And Jack Simpson downed an entire mug of beer and ordered another one. The others just stared back with wide eyes.

Dad resumed the story.

"Frank said 'I only did a partial castration. He still has another one. Let's take him to the hospital. We can tell everybody he had an emergency hernia operation, which is kinda true because he did have a hernia. You would have had to operate on him in a couple of weeks anyway.'

'What wrong with keeping him here for a few days,' Frank suggested after a moment.

'For one thing he is going to wake up eventually. The other thing is that people might wonder where the sheriff is. He probably has not been seen or heard from for several hours.'

We dodged a bullet on the second thing. Frank made up some issues about cows escaping on FM 1174 and called the Sheriff's office to speak to the sheriff. Delores, who worked the desk, told him the sheriff was up around Benchley for the whole afternoon and wouldn't be back until after six, but she would send a deputy.

After a second shot of Jack Daniels, I told Frank the hospital idea might work. We could fill out the admittance work since it was an emergency. Since it was almost five o'clock by then we decided to wait until dark to transport him to the county hospital.

We took a couple more shots of whiskey and then Frank and I wrapped him up in the sheets and toted him out to Frank's pickup truck. We decided to go in his vehicle because he had a bed of hay and some horse blankets in the back. Oh, I forgot to say that I gave the sheriff another shot of anesthesia – human kind.

We got to the ER just after dark that night. We loaded him onto a gurney and rolled him inside. As expected, Maggie Lou Dowling was working the night shift. I'll never forget how big her brown eyes got when she saw who was on the stretcher. I looked at her and said "The sheriff had an accident. Good thing Frank and I were there. Give Frank the admission papers to fill out and let's get the sheriff a room." Maggie Lou had worked the ER night admissions at the county hospital for almost 20 years and had seen enough to know there are some things never to be mentioned in polite company.

Me, Frank, and Maggie Lou took the sheriff into a private room and Maggie Lou hooked him up to an IV. The first thing I did was inject a dose of that 'do not remember' drug into the IV tube and hoped he didn't remember much if anything.

Soon as Maggie Lou and I got him into a room, I called my wife, Ruthie, to let her know I would be later than usual. I told her the sheriff had an emergency hernia operation, but he was fine.

Frank called the sheriff's department to let them know and they notified Cooper's sister in Carthage since she was listed as next of kin. I knew by Thursday morning between my wife, the Baptist Church prayer chain and the sheriff's department everyone in the county and all surrounding ones would know the official story.

I slipped him another dose of pain killer into his IV and hoped he would sleep until 7 in the morning. I also left instructions with Maggie Lou to either give him another dose or call me, depending on what time it was.

Maggie Lou called me about 7:15 the next morning and said she was getting off her shift and that the sheriff was awake.

I called Frank. He said he was on his way to the Terrill place to deliver a calf but would be there as soon as possible.

Cooper was pretty calm when I arrived. He asked what happened and I started telling him the story Frank and I agreed upon. I said, "You tripped on a rock and your gun discharged and grazed you in the gluteus maximus. When you were admitted to the Emergency Room, I noticed you also had a hernia about to burst, so I went ahead and fixed it. He was okay with that. I told him he would be fine and could probably go home the day after tomorrow. I told him that due to the hernia location, it was necessary to perform a partial gonadectomy. Cooper looked alarmed and said, "A what?"

Just then Frank busted through the door and said, "It's also called an orchiectomy. It means one of your cajones is missing."

That is when I realized I did not give Cooper enough of the 'do not remember' drug. He was furious. He began to call Frank every name you could think have, threatened to kill both of us, called our mother you-know-what, and tried to get out of the bed to come after Frank. He screamed he was going to sue Frank, me, the hospital, and anybody he could think of.

Frank just laughed and looked at him straight in the eyes and said 'You know Texas law. I will say I saw you and my wife, and it was a crime of passion. My defense will be I was overcome with extreme emotion and just couldn't control my actions. You know the jury will let me off. Besides, if you take this to court your private parts will be shown to the jury, the press and everybody in the courthouse in living color. You might want to think about that before getting a lawyer and going to court. Here, I bought you this plant from the lobby. The desk is filled with flowers for you. I think this is an orchid - to go with your orchiotomy.'

By this time, Cooper was asleep again due to the shot of sleepy I put in his IV. Just as Frank and I were about to leave the room, two volunteer Candy Stripers opened the door bringing two more plants. I took one, and as I was putting it on the window ledge, I noticed the typing on the card said, 'Ronald O.B. Cooper.' When I looked at the second plant, the name on the card was also 'Ronald O.B. Cooper.'

I looked at Frank who was grinning like the old Cheshire cat. I sighed and asked 'Frank? What have you done now?'

'You told me to fill out the admission papers, so I did. I listed his name as Ronald O.B. Cooper. Then I called Beverly at the Floral Shop to tell her that all flowers and plants ordered for the Sheriff should be addressed with O. B. because there was another Ronald Cooper in the hospital.'

By the time he was released from the hospital, everybody was calling O. B. thinking that was part of his given name. He decided the best way to deal with the nickname was to adopt it and go with it. And that is how Sheriff Ronald Cooper became known as Obie."

Everybody began to laugh except Joseph Linwood.

He said, "I don't get it."

This made everyone laugh even more.

Dad looked at Joe and said "Well, the "O" stood for 'One' and if you cannot figure out what the "B" was for, then I will bring you a poster of the male anatomy."

The light bulb hit Joseph about that time. He started laughing so hard he had to pull out his inhaler again.

We all raised our mugs to raise a final farewell toast to Obie Cooper and soon left the lodge. Dad and I took the long way back to the facility enjoying the afternoon sun. When we walked into his room, I could tell he had enjoyed himself to the fullest.

When he was settled in, I said, "Dad, that was a great story you told. How much of it was true?"

He looked at me, got out of his recliner and stepped into the small closet. When he returned, he grinned and placed an old Mason jar on the table in front of me and said, "All of it." I almost fainted.

The Wedding of the Decade

Every other Thursday at 4:00 pm, the three Thibideaux girls and I walked to Mrs. Weaver's for tea and crumpets. Nina Thibideaux and I were seniors at Flora High School and best friends. Her two sisters, Dora Mae and Doris were a junior and a freshman, respectively.

None of us liked hot tea and we had no idea what crumpets were, but we liked to call our get-togethers tea and crumpets because we had seen the fancy people from England in a magazine having them. We had lemonade and cookies or cake.

Mrs. Weaver thought it was important for girls to learn proper manners. I suppose balancing a glass of lemonade and a plate of cookies on your lap without dumping the whole thing on the floor was important before going out into the world in 1931.

My Daddy and the Thibideaux sisters' daddy worked at the Pumping Station in Flora, Louisiana. Mrs. Weaver's husband, Burton, owned the sawmill. Those two places employed most of the people who lived in Flora.

It was the first Thursday in March, and we arrived on time. I enjoyed sitting in the parlor with Mrs. Weaver and the girls. It made me feel grown up.

After we were seated and sipping our lemonade, Mrs. Weaver asked "Do you girls have dates for the dance a week from Saturday? You know it's the dance when a girl asks a fellow?"

Nina immediately said "Of course! I asked J.L. Lewis, and he said yes."

Everybody in town knew those two were sweet on each other. Dora Mae said she planned to ask Tom Baker, and Doris said she intended to ask Tom's twin brother Edward.

Everybody turned and looked at me for an answer.

I took the last sip of my lemonade and said, "I am not going. I do not know any boy I would want to go with."

"Oh, but you must," they responded in chorus. "It will be your last chance to ask someone before you graduate in May."

I set my glass and plate on the coffee table.

"There is no one in town I am interested in," I said with a snobbish sniff.

"How about that new bookkeeper Burton hired at the sawmill a month ago?" Mrs. Weaver suggested.

"I heard he has a girlfriend from up around Colfax," I replied as a matter of fact. "One of the O'Quinn girls," I added for emphasis.

"Come on Doy, it is just a dance. It's not like you are going to marry him. Isn't his name Randall?" Dora Mae said.

I took a deep breath and replied, "I've seen him, and he is too skinny. No wonder they call him Slats. If he turned sideways, he would be invisible."

"Sounds like you already checked him out," Mrs. Weaver smiled. "He stays here at the boarding house, and he is very polite. I think you should ask him."

"He doesn't know me from a rabbit hole in the ground, and I would be so embarrassed if he said no."

"But he might say yes. You would never know unless you ask him," Nina said.

"Well, I will think about it," I said.

"No, I think you should go down to the Commissary tomorrow after school and ask him. I insist," Mrs. Weaver said. "I'll tell Burton to tell him to be up front at 4:00. You can ask him then."

Nina, Dora Mae, and Doris looked at me with demanding eyes. I knew it was four against one.

The next afternoon, Nina walked with me to the Commissary to ensure I would actually ask him. I wore a bright yellow dress with little white daisies, and I let Nina fix my hair in a wave. We were both going to beauty school in Natchitoches when we graduated. I put on some lipstick and rouge, but not enough to look painted. She waited outside on the porch. I took a deep breath, opened the screen door, and went inside.

As promised, there he was standing behind the counter. He was talking to Mr. Groves and Mr. Weaver. As soon as I walked in, both of them went to the back of the store leaving Randall alone. I was certain they were within ear shot.

"Hello," he said.

"Hello, my name is Doy Faust."

"I know. You are Mr. Ed Faust's oldest daughter, right?" He opened the swinging gate that separated the counter from the front of the store and came to stand face to face with me.

He was slightly over six feet tall, with dark black hair and brown eyes with gold flecks in the iris. He wore rimless spectacles with gold earpieces. It made him look very smart.

He smiled a crooked smile and said, "I do not think I have ever heard the name Doy. It is odd."

"Not as odd as my first name. It is Exa."

He looked deep into my eyes and said "Exa? I know I have never heard that name before."

"My father's cousin is named Doy. Two weeks before he was to get married his fiancée was killed in an automobile accident near Pineville. It was two weeks before I was born. She was named Exa, so I was named after both of them."

"Hmm. Well, your names are unique. So, you must be unique too."

I did not know what to say to that, so I stammered, "I was wondering if you had a date for the dance, next Saturday?" I was so nervous I was about to pass out.

"No," was all he said, but he smiled, and his eyes twinkled behind the lens of his glasses.

"Well, would you like to go with me?" I could not believe I said it.

He did not answer.

I was about to turn and walk out the door, when he said, "I would. I am going to help with the play the Methodist men are putting on, but that is before the dance. We could meet at the church afterwards and walk to the schoolhouse."

I smiled and said, "That will be fine. I am going to the play. I will see you there."

As soon as Nina saw my face, she knew he had said yes. We skipped all the way to Mrs. Weaver's house to let her know. I don't know why I was feeling so happy. It was just a date to a dance.

When we got to Mrs. Weaver's, she served Coca-Cola over ice and fresh lemon squares. I told her he said yes but was helping with the play just before the dance.

Mrs. Weaver said "Oh, everybody in town will either be at the play or be in the play. This is the first time the Methodist Men's Group have put on the womanless wedding. All of the actors are men! It is called *The Wedding of the Decade*. Burton and I saw one in New Orleans, and it was hysterical. All of the prominent men in town will be in it. Burton is going to be the master of ceremonies and Little Burton is going to be the ring bearer. Richard Smith is going to be the groom. I hear the mother of the bride is a big surprise."

Nina said "Richard Smith is the shortest person in Flora at five-foot-six-inches and he has that long gray beard that is almost down to his waist. I heard Swen Johansson is going to be the bride. He stands six-foot-five-inches and has red hair and a red beard. They should be a hoot."

"What part did Randall say he was going to be?" Mrs. Weaver asked.

"I did not ask him. He just said he was helping with the play. I guess we will be surprised."

The week before the dance seemed to drag on like the summer heat. I decided to wear the green dress with the white collar I made in home economics class. The fabric color matched my eyes just perfectly.

The parking lot of the Methodist Church was filled with cars, horses and buggies when my family and I arrived about 5:45. We each paid our twenty-five-cent admission and went inside the church. The church was filled to the rafters. I immediately spied Nina and went to sit with her. We were Baptists and the only times I had been in the Methodist Church was when I sometimes went with Nina and once to the christening for the Burnside baby. I really could not tell a big difference between the two churches other than we did a full dunking baptism while the Methodist settled for a sprinkling.

Nina and I sat on the end of a pew near the back. The church was full. They opened the Sunday School rooms at the back and put up folding chairs for the overflow.

At 6:00, Mr. Weaver stepped to the middle of the altar.

"Ladies and Gentlemen," he began. "Welcome to the Methodist Men's fund raiser – *The Wedding of the Decade*. I will be your master of ceremonies and announcing the wedding party as they join us. First, let us welcome the preacher, Flora Mayor, Parish Sheriff, and now Preacher – Sam James."

People clapped and the newly appointed Preacher James took his place at the alter and Mr. Weaver stepped to the side. James wore a long, black robe he borrowed from a judge in Natchitoches and carried Volume S of the Encyclopedia Britannica.

Leona Spencer, the only woman in the play, slowly crept up the stairs behind the pulpit and took her place at the piano just as

Mr. Weaver said, "Our music for the evening is presented by Miss Leona Spencer."

A few folks laughed because Miss Leona was sometimes called Leona Spinster because her only beau was killed in the War Between the States. She had more years on her than the piano had keys. And with 88 keys, she sometimes got 44 of them in the correct order when she played.

She began to play *Oh my darling, oh my darling, oh my darling, Clementine,* as Mr. Weaver said, "Let us welcome the mother of the groom, the lovely Clementine, and father of the groom, the handsome Cletus Smith. The groom's mother was played by Clem Smith who was foreman at the sawmill planer mill. He had on a bright purple satin dress with a pink flower headpiece that looked more like earmuffs in his brown hair. Clem was short and fat, so he resembled a giant grape with legs walking down the aisle followed by a bean pole, Cletus Jackson. Mr. Jackson had on his only suit. He said he bought it for weddings and funerals, including his when it happened.

Leona hit about five correct notes in a row switching to *On Top of Old Smokey* as Mr. Weaver said, "And now here comes the lovely mother of the bride, Mrs. Josephine Thornton." The crowd went crazy and was hooting and hollering as the exceptionally large, very red faced, very old, very white-haired minister of the Baptist church, Joseph Thornton, appeared. He was wearing one of the robin egg blue choir robes and carrying a bouquet of yellow daffodils. Nina and I could not believe the preacher had on rouge and lipstick. He swished down the aisle causing the choir robe to swing back and forth over his large behind like waves in the ocean.

Above the escalating laughter, Mr. Weaver continued, "Escorting the first beautiful bridesmaid is Tom Baker with Miss Bootsie May Morgan."

Bootsie had on a red and white striped sun dress that showed all of the black hair on his chest and on his forearms. He wore a straw sun bonnet with a red rose attached that belong to his aunt Mildred. He carried a red Cali lily.

Tom had on his black suit and he and Bootsie walked down the aisle. They separated when they reached the altar. Before sitting on the front row, Bootsie May scratched his behind sending the audience into uncontrolled fits of laughing. Tom was laughing so hard he almost tripped when he took his place in front of the kneeling rail.

Mr. Weaver continued, "Following Tom is Edward Baker with our second bridesmaid, the lovely Norma Dent."

Norm Dent also worked at the pumping station with Daddy. His dress was identical to Bootsie's except it was blue and white striped. The two looked almost identical except Norm had a full gray beard. He carried a bouquet of yellow daffodils that clashed with his dress.

Leona changed the music to something almost recognizable when Mr. Weaver announced, "The beautiful maid of honor, Phillipia Youngblood, is escorted by the best man, Tom Duckworth."

Phillip Youngblood, who everybody called Skeeter, had on a rose-colored taffeta and satin ballgown with lace that looked left over from the Confederacy. On his head he wore a large white crocheted doily that fell just below his ears with pink daffodils pinned to it with bobbi pins. The pink made his black mustache look even darker over his brightly painted red lips.

"Now comes our ring bearer, Burton Weaver, Jr."

Like all the other true men in the wedding he had on a black suit carrying a pillow. I wondered where the men dressed as women found shoes the size of their big feet. And did every man own a black suit?

Everybody was howling at all the characters and their shenanigans as each came down the aisle and took their places.

Mr. Weaver said, "And last, but before the bride is our precious little flower girl, Miss Randella Duffey."

Just as Randall or now Randalla, reached the pew where Nina and I were sitting, he stopped and smiled at me. He had blacked out his two front teeth. He was wearing a baby blue polka dot dress that reached only to mid-thigh. His head was covered with a matching blue hat with tiny white flowers pinned to it. He carried a white wicker basket with a pink bow that filled with pink carnations that matched the sash on his dress.

Nina almost fell off the pew laughing. I slapped her on the arm, jumped over her and ran out the door of the church just as the bride was about to walk down the aisle. I ran all the way up the hill and did not stop until I stepped onto my front porch. I was glad my family was still at the wedding, and I had the house to myself to calm down. How embarrassing. There was no way I was going to go to the dance with the flower girl.

About 7:15 my parents and my two sisters returned. They were all still laughing as they entered the living room.

"How did you get home so fast?" asked my younger sister, Claudia. "Nina said you left early, but we did not know when. You did see Mr. Johansson come down the aisle as the bride? He had on a veil that kept sticking to his red beard. His belly stuck out like he was pregnant."

"Claudia! We don't use that word. We say, 'with child,'" Daddy scolded her. Claudie rolled her eyes in the back of her head.

Marjorie, who was ten, said, "It was so funny when the bride and bridesmaids picked up the groom and the groomsmen and carried them down the aisle as Miss Leona played the *Stars and Stripes Forever*. The flower girl picked up Little Burton and tossed him over his shoulder like a bag of flour. Aunt Alice laughed so hard she peed in her pants making a puddle on the floor right next to me."

With that I jumped and ran to the bedroom and slammed the door.

A few minutes later there was a knock on the door. Daddy entered when I said come in. He sat on the bed beside me.

"What's wrong, Honey?" he asked.

I leaned into his shoulder and said "I was so embarrassed when I saw him as the flower girl. When I saw those sticks, he calls legs and those doorknobs for knees I ran out of the church. I am not going to the dance with him."

"Oh, Honey," he said as he put his arm around me. "It was all in fun. I am sure he did not mean any harm. The Methodist Men probably made over $150. They will use it to do good things for the church and for Flora. With Preacher Thornton playing a part in it I heard the Methodist are going to give some money to the Baptist

Church to actually put in a baptismal font, so we won't have to go to Mill Creek and worry about snakes."

"I don't care, Daddy. I'm not going."

Just then, Claudia and Margorie stuck their heads in the door. "The flower girl is here to see you," they cried in unison, laughing.

"Tell him to go away," I said.

Daddy said, "Now, Honey, at least go say hello to him and tell him to his face you do not want to go. It would be the polite thing to do."

I never wanted to disappoint my daddy, so I took a deep breath, stood up and straightened my dress. I made a quick glance in the mirror and ran a brush through my hair.

I opened the screen door and there stood Mr. Randall Duffey dressed in the most beautiful while linen suit I had ever seen. His white shirt was starched so stiffly I thought it might break. He held a straw hat in his hands with a black satin hatband that perfectly

matched his silk tie that boasted a rhinestone stickpin. His black

shoes were so highly polished they almost glowed. I was speechless.

He stepped forward and asked with a shy, crooked smile

revealing beautiful white teeth, "Would you like to go out with me,

now?"

I married him the following February.

The Royal Order of the Daughters of Hernia

(pronounced Her NEEN ia)

Gertrude Harriet McMillan was born in 1927 at her parent's house in Cut Cross, Texas. After her little brother was born two years later, he was unable to say 'Gertrude' and called her Tood. It wasn't long before Tood became Toody and stuck forever.

Toody was everything one imagined about a west Texas frontier woman. She was brazened, bold, independent, and tenacious. And she was only 5-feet-4-inches tall.

Her grandfather raised the finest Hereford cattle in the state on one of the largest ranches in the Texas Panhandle. Her father was President of the Union Pacific Railroad that ensured the cattle went to market.

After high school, Toody attended Southern Methodist University in Dallas to which her grandfather had donated buckets of money. At SMU, Toody majored in Pi Beta Phi social sorority and being Homecoming Queen. Even though Toody was one of the most popular girls on campus, she seldom dated. When she absolutely needed a date, she ensured her gay friend, Roy, President of Phi Delta Theta, was available. Somehow, she managed to obtain a degree in business administration.

After Toody graduated from SMU, her father moved the family from the Panhandle to Hearne, Texas to become chief executive officer of the Missouri Pacific Railroad. Even though it increased the family income significantly, Toody hated it. She was angry that her brother stayed in West Texas to run their grandfather's ranch. Even after her father built her mother and Toody a ranch house, complete with guest cottage right out of Architectural Digest, she thought Hearne was the ugliest town she had ever seen and that included many awful places in West Texas.

One weekend in 1950, Toody invited her high school sweetheart, Oscar, down from West Texas. Neither of them had seen much of each other since high school. Oscar had attended The

Agricultural and Mechanical College of Texas and had been an all-

conference quarterback. He graduated with a degree that had

something to do with cows. At Saturday morning breakfast, Toody

announced to her parents that she and Oscar were engaged and

would be moving back to West Texas to get married.

Toody's father, smiled, looked at Oscar and said, "If I offered

the two of you 500 acres of good farm and ranch land and a few

head of prime cattle with a heritage and pedigree as a wedding gift,

would you change your mind about moving back to West Texas?"

It was a game-changing offer.

It was the largest and fanciest wedding in Hearne, Texas.

Toody McMillan became the bride of Oscar Byrd IV and Toody Byrd

became a force to be reckoned with.

The marriage of Toody and Oscar was like the marriage of

two old kingdoms. Money married money and made more money.

They raised two perfect children, a boy, and a girl, who married

perfect spouses, and each had two perfect children for a total of

four perfect grandchildren who lived in Dallas and Houston,

respectively. They lived a happy life.

Toody and Oscar were seldom seen in public without their

life-long friends. Two of Toody's Pi Phi sisters, Ethel and Gloria, and

their husbands often attended Toody and Oscar's charity functions.

In fact, the two couples built weekend homes near Toody and Oscar.

Eventually, Ethel and Gloria spent more time in Hearne than in

Dallas. And rounding out the group was Margo Bell, Oscar's sister

and thus Toody's sister-in-law.

It was at the 1977 Annual Dip & Spit Golf Tournament at the

Country Club that Oscar suddenly dropped dead on the golf course

one Saturday afternoon. Toody was in the bar sipping on her second

margarita with her girlfriends when Oscar's golf buddies came to tell

her the news.

Her first response was "Had he putted out? Oscar never likes to leave things unfinished."

When they said, "Yes, and he scored a birdie on Hole 14," she gulped the remains her margarita and said, "Well, take me home, Boys. Let's get the grieving started."

As girlfriends, Ethel and Gloria rushed to comfort their friend, Margo grabbed her husband, Freddie Bell and asked, "What the Hell? We saw an ambulance leave over an hour ago. What took you guys so long to come tell her?"

Freddie shook his arm loose and said, "We played on to finish eighteen. We thought Oscar would have wanted that."

It would be several months before Toody and the town realized that Toody Byrd was now the wealthiest widow in Robertson County and ranked in the top five wealthy widows of Texas.

Life after Oscar was good for Toody Byrd. Of course, there were many suitors, but Toody was smart enough to know that old men were looking for a nurse or a purse. She was not the bed-pan-emptying type and her purse was just that – hers. . And it had a padlock on it.

Toody used her money to do good things around Hearne. She got the Annual Dip and Spit Golf Tournament renamed to the Oscar Byrd Memorial Tournament with proceeds going to the American Heart Association.

Toody's annual Christmas Fund Raiser raised money for, as she would say, "the orphans and afflicted."

The invitation-only event was the highlight of the Christmas season. And of course, coming from a family of Yellow-Dog Democrats she always wrote a big check to the Democratic Party. And if anyone needed help, Toody was there to help regardless of social standing, race, or religion.

Despite Oscar dropping dead on the golf course at The Hearne Country Club, Toody maintained the membership. She and her three girlfriends always had dinner there on Tuesdays, when it was Tex-Mex Buffet with half price pitchers of margaritas, and Fridays when it was all you eat boiled shrimp plus fried catfish. And of course, Happy Hour priced margarita pitchers.

It was after either the Tuesday Tex-Mex Buffet with margaritas or the Friday Happy Hour with shrimp and margaritas, that Toody and her three girlfriends, Ethel, Gloria, and Margo declared themselves The Royal Order of the Daughters of Hernia (pronounced Her NEEN ia). With Toody unanimously declared as Founder, they would provide support for the community.

It was on the way home from a Tex-Mex Buffet Happy Hour one summer that Toody and the Daughters of Hernia were pulled over by a local officer. Of course, it was only 6:30 in the evening and still hours away from sunset.

When the large Black man approached her silver Mercedes, Toody rolled down her window and said, "I am Toody Byrd. And you are?"

He was somewhat taken aback, but grinned and in a deep baritone voice replied, "I am the new Deputy Sheriff. My name is Dewey Daah."

Before he could respond, Toody continued, "Yes, I heard the town was getting more law enforcements. I am so glad. Welcome. Tell me about your people. Where are you from? Your last name is Daah with two of the letter A. How unusual."

"Mrs. Byrd?" Dewey tried again. "Do you realize you just drove out of the Country Club and through the ditch?"

Toody replied, "Why yes, I have done it before, so I know my car will make it. Except of course if there is a flood or something."

Just then Ethel rolled down the back window, leaned out and threw up her cheese enchiladas that gave off a mild odor of tequila.

Toody smiled and immediately said, "Food poisoning, I bet."

Dewey had already been briefed on Toody and the Daughters, and he did not want to be the one giving the town's wealthiest patrons and her friends a DUI on his first day of work.

"Ladies, you seemed to be having a bit of trouble. May I assist in getting you safely home?"

"Don't do it," Margo screamed. "We do not know who his people are, and he wants to follow you."

"Shut up Margo. Stop being such a Republican," Toody said. She then said to the officer, "I will be happy to have you follow me. I just live down the road a piece." In fact, it was exactly two miles to the front gate of Toody's residence.

Daah replied, "Yes, Ma'am. I know where you live."

He returned to his car, flashed his blue lights, and allowed Toody to pull out ahead of him. He followed them safely to her ranch and watched them safely maneuver through the black wrought iron gate leading to the Byrd mansion where he hoped the others would sober up enough to drive home.

As Toody pulled into her circular driveway, she turned to her friends and said, "That new officer is named Dewey Daah. So that means he is Deputy Dew Daah!"

The Daughters of Hernia howled with laughter and peed in their Depends.

As luck would have it, after that night, Toody Byrd and Deputy Dew Daah became the best of friends. It was Deputy Daah that was first on the scene when on her way to water aerobics one morning Toody ran off the road, through the ditch, through a barbed wire fence with the Mercedes landing under a billboard just narrowly missing the support posts.

Deputy Dew Daah was on the scene in minutes. He ran his car through the ditch and over the broken fence and pulled up next to Toody's car. He yanked opened the door only to hear Toody say, "Bout time. Get me out of here."

Dewey replied, "No way, Toody. Not until the ambulance and fire truck arrive. Here they come now."

"I don't need an ambulance!" Toody insisted.

"Yes, you do, Toody. You need to be checked out. You might have had a stroke or a heart attack."

"I did not have a stroke or a heart attack," Toody said vehemently. "I was looking at that damn sign." When the fireman reached Toody and released the seat belt she jumped out of the car, pointed up and screamed, "What in the Devil's name is that? Who put that up there?"

"Calm down Toody," Deputy Dew Daah said, "Your head is bleeding. You might be in shock. You might have had a stroke. Or a heart attack?"

"Shut up Dew, I am not in shock, and I already told you I did not have a stroke or a heart attack. I lost control of the car when I saw that billboard, she screamed. "Who is THAT? That... that ... THAT HUSSY! And why is it up there?"

The giant billboard overlooking the highway had a headshot of a highly made-up woman, wearing bright Jungle Red lipstick with a diamond encrusted crown on her head like a queen. To the side of the giant picture against a gold background written in red lettering was the name, "Brenda Jo Wyatt, New Owner of Datsun Motor Company."

Ethel and Gloria arrived at the ER first, with Margo arriving a few minutes later. At the ER Toody received three butterfly stitches over her right eye, and she boasted a shiner that would make Muhammed Ali proud.

Two days later, Toody, Ethel and Gloria met Margo at the Country Club for the Friday Happy Hour of shrimp and margaritas.

Just as the second pitcher of margaritas arrived, Gloria looked up and said, "What tha'?" They turned to see a strange woman of indeterminate age, wearing a shining silver sequined top over black jeans almost gliding toward their table in bright red stiletto heels. Her expensive perfume preceded her by only seconds.

Before any of them could speak, she said in a bad Marilyn Monroe husky voice, "I am so sorry to interrupt, but I saw you ladies sitting here and I just had to come and meet you. I am , Brenda Jo Wyatt of the Houston Wyatts."

Toody, calm as always, said, "How do you do? I am Toody Byrd, and these are my dearest friends, Ethel, Gloria, and Margo."

She cast a quick glance toward the other three and focused on Toody, "I so wanted to meet you, Toody. May I call you, Toody since we just met? I am in a major rush at the moment, but I wanted to tell you that I am looking forward to one of those Christmas invitations of yours. I'll be bringing my checkbook."

She gushed, "And I have Christmas trees throughout my home in Houston all decorated with Christmas trees from Neiman Marcus. I would just love to see how you decorate out here in the country. I do hope to see you soon and visit more. I am so busy being a businesswoman, you know."

She retreated and glided out as quickly as she had glided in, leaving the Daughters of Hernia speechless.

Ethel was refilling the glasses emptying the pitcher and Gloria was ordering another one, when Margo said, "Well, she looked at us like we had dog poop on our noses."

"Well, she sure looked down her nose job nose at us, didn't she?" said Ethel. And the Daughters' statements began to flow faster than the tequila going down their throats.

"I have not worn that much make-up in one week."

"I think those jeans were painted on. Is it appropriate to wear sequins before dark?"

"I heard she married, divorced that Japanese car dealer, and took him for everything he had. Didn't even leave him a toothbrush when she moved out. I wonder whose husband she is going after in Hearne."

"How old do you think she is?"

"Somewhere between 50 and 100."

"No woman her age has that much hair."

"Do you think that bosom is real? I don't think there is anything real about her."

"I think I know why the hospital just got a plastic surgeon."

After the initial meeting, as one might suspect, the two women moved in different circles. They rarely saw each other. All went well until Toody turned her wall calendar from September 30 to October 1. There on the first day of October was her reminder to make the reservations for the Grand Ball Room for the Daughters' Annual Christmas party at the Country Club. When she called, she was told that every Saturday in December was taken. Despite Toody's attempts to inform the young clerk that the second Saturday in December is always reserved for the Daughters' Annual Christmas Party, he was adamant that there was no mistake. That Saturday was already booked. Toody lost her religion twice with the new person and once with the Manager of the Country Club.

When Toody threatened to withdraw her membership if the manager did not tell her who booked that weekend, he told her "Brenda Jo Wyatt. It is booked as her engagement announcement."

Toody hung up on him and called an emergency meeting of The Royal Order of the Daughters of Hernia.

Gloria arrived first with two bottles of Chardonnay, a box Ritz Crackers and a tub of cream cheese. She said it was all she had at the moment's notice. Margo and Ethel arrived each carrying a canvas grocery bag in each hand filled with enough alcohol and snacks to soothe whatever problems lay ahead of them.

As the first glasses of wine were poured, Toody told them

the whole story of the mix-up of dates at the Country Club.

The first round was filled with comments of shock,

sympathy, and anger and questions of "what do we do?" And most

of all speculation about Brenda Jo Wyatt's engagement party.

"Monty Heatherton is a very recent widower," said Gloria.

Ethel replied, "Y'all know that Monty's wife, well, she was

still his wife because the divorce papers had not been signed. So,

they were still married when the accident happened, and she ran

run up under that 18-wheeler."

Margo said, "So sad. Penny not even cold in the ground. Just

10 months ago and him already remarrying."

When the second round was poured, Margo tossed the

newspaper on the table and said, "Look at this! In today's paper!"

It was with a picture and headline that read "Brenda Jo

Wyatt becomes city's most social socialite."

The photo showed Brenda Jo surrounded by women wearing long ball gown dresses and large hats with feathers from birds that died in vain. The caption read, "Brenda Jo Wyatt revives the afternoon tea party."

Margo huffed, "That picture of her looks like she is a queen holding court with her ladies in waiting."

By the third round and opening of a second bottle, the comments shifted to referring to Brenda Jo in terms of a female dog. By the time the second bottle was emptied, the Daughters were referring to Brenda Jo Wyatt in terms of incestual family relationships with the family matriarch.

Throughout most of the Brenda Jo bashing Toody sat in deep thought. She glanced at the newspaper still lying on the table and saw the article next to Brenda Jo's Tea Party. It was an article about the removal of the old tennis courts at the Country Club. New tennis courts had been completed in the summer. These two regulation size courts were to be destroyed and the area repaved to provide more parking.

Suddenly, Toody cried, "I have a scathingly brilliant idea!" By the end of the third bottle of wine The Daughters of Hernia had an action plan designed and ready to execute. The fourth bottle was simply to celebrate their achievement.

Two weeks before Thanksgiving, The Daughters placed a full-page ad in the Hearne Herald announcing the First Annual Christmas Cow Plop Bingo Fund Raiser to be held on the Second Saturday of December at the Hearne Country Club. The ad went on to describe entry fees for those who wanted to sponsor a cow, ticket prices for those who wanted to attend, ticket prices for those who wanted to wager on cows and of course the location. The event was to be held at the Hearne Country Club on the old tennis courts next to the restaurant and the ballroom.

When Brenda Jo Wyatt saw it, she picked up a lamp and threw it through the plate glass door of the kitchen. The paper carried the full-page notice in the Wednesday and Saturday editions. Brenda Jo Wyatt tended to break something each time she saw it.

The Friday before the Cow Plop Bingo was to take place, Toody and a few others were on the local morning radio show.

People tuned in to hear, "Good morning friends and neighbors. This here is old Ed Morris with Station WHRN, 620 on your AM dial. I am out and about in the Old Yeller Van and today we are at the Hearne Country Club where we have Ms. Toody Byrd and six cow wranglers to tell us about the First Annual Christmas Cow Plop Bingo Fundraiser.

"Toody? Let's start with you. You have always hosted a Christmas party that raised funds on the second Saturday of December, but this year you are hosting the First Annual Christmas Cow Plop Bingo. Why did you change?"

Toody laughed, "Well, you know, Ed. There is so much manure, as polite people say, in the world today. As our town grows and others move here, they tend to bring a great deal of manure. We might as well put it to good use, have a little fun, and hopefully raised some funds to help in town projects."

"Tell us how it all got started," said Ed.

"We asked for local businesses to sponsor a cow. We have six sponsors. Each sponsor paid $1000 to enter a cow. Then they picked these Cow Wranglers, as I call 'em, to participate in Cow Plop Bingo."

"Let's visit with these Wranglers really quickly and then come back to you Toody and you can tell us how this works."

"You, Sir. Tell us your name, your cow's name and who sponsored you." Ed put the microphone toward the first fellow. "Howdy, I am T. J. Jacoby and my cow's name is Mudpie and our sponsor is Buckley Chevrolet. Ed moved the microphone to the next man who said, "My name is Jason McNeil, and my cow is Suzi Q sponsored by Dawson and Sons Meat Market. Ed went on down the line. There was Cody Davis with Brownie sponsored by the Dairy Queen, Billy Joe Henderson with Honey sponsored by Gleason Motor Repair, Wayne Shepard sponsored by the City Café with Peachie Pie, and Bubba Stephens sponsored by Henry's Hideaway with a cow named Cynthia.

"I understand Peach Pie is a contest winner. Is that correct?" Ed asked Wayne.

"Yes, Miss Peachie Pie here won first place in a cow plop bingo over in Onalaska last spring. Got a trophy too!" Ed turned the microphone to another wrangle and said, "And you, Billie Joe, I believe you said you are here with Honey? Have you done anything to train or assist Honey with her responsibilities?"

"Well, I been feeding her really good. You know a cow poops 12 to 15 times a day. We are hoping for a quick plop that gives a winner."

"Now, Toody, this event is at the old tennis courts right by the club house, right? How does this work?"

"Yes, the old tennis complex is going to be destroyed. It is the perfect place to hold the Cow Plop Bingo. There are two regulation sized tennis courts, side by side and separated by a 12-foot chain-link fence. The stands have not been torn down and the lights still work, and the construction fencing is already in place for the demolition to take place. On the second court, we put up some temporary bleachers, some refreshment tents and tables where individuals can purchase the few remaining spaces on the bingo cards. People can see through the fence and into the first court.

On the first court we pieced together two very large black plastic tarps. Then we painted a giant bingo card on the tarp. At the appointed time, two cows will take the court for Round One of the contest. Each cow is timed. The first to make her deposit on a square is the winner of that round. People can bid on one, two or all three rounds. There are several ways to win. One can wager on the cow, or one can wager on the square where the cow makes her deposit."

"What does a winner receive?" asked Ed.

"If your wager is a winner, you receive a $10 gift certificate from Dick's Cut-Rate Liquor and a free oil change from Buckley Chevrolet. Each sponsor of the three cows receives a trophy, donated by Jackson's Trophy House and each wrangler receives a $25 gift certificate donated by Harris Western Wear."

Ed asked, "How do you determine first, second and third place?"

"It is based on the time it takes for the deposit to be made," Toody laughed. "So y'all put on your you-know-what kickers, come on out, have some fun, and help raise some funds for the city of Hearne.

During the live on-air broadcast, Brenda Jo called the radio station three times and chewed out a young receptionist who had no idea what Brenda Jo was talking about. After that, she did two shots of tequila, even thought it was only 10:30 in the morning.

December weather in Texas can be tricky. It can be a calm and pleasant 68 degrees or a freezing sleet storm. Sometimes both, on the same day. As luck would have it, the second Saturday in December was a beautiful crystal-clear night. By 7:00 pm the stands of the old tennis courts were filled, and the temporary bleachers were filled for the 8:00 start. There was standing room only. One could hear the cows mooing and fans cheering.

The first round with Mudpie and Peach Pie went very quickly, with both contestants making quick deposits. However, Peach Pie was timed at one minute and six seconds on Square N 52 with Mudpie depositing at one minute and fifteen seconds on O 72. However, neither cow deposited on a winning square. The deposits were scooped up and placed in a five-gallon bucket.

The second round between Brownie and Suzie Q took a bit more time. Both cows wandered across the tarps. Brownie caused a roar of excitement when she raised her tail, but she only peed. It was then that Suzie Q took her cue and deposited it on the B10 square at a time of two minutes and eight seconds.

The final round boasted Honey and Cynthia. As soon as the two cows were released Cynthia wandered to the O 58 square and made an immediate deposit in seven seconds."

The Hearne Herald took a photo of Cynthia, Bubba Stevens, the wrangler, Henry and the owner of Henry's Hideaway.

When asked how Cynthia got her name, Bubba smiled and said, "After my mother-in-law."

By midnight, the first and what became the only Christmas Cow Plop Bingo was over. The guests were gone, the tarps had been rolled up and packed into the back of a pick-up truck and the pick-up trucks pulling cow trailers were gone. Deputy Dewey Daah worked traffic at the Country Club that night.

On Monday, Deputy Sheriff Dewey Daah knocked on Toody's door about 10:30 in the morning. Toody invited him in but was surprised when he said that he was there in "an official capacity." Nevertheless, he followed Toody to her kitchen and sat down at the table.

Toody poured them both a cup of coffee, sat Dewey's in front of him and took a seat opposite him. "What kind of official capacity are you here for, Dew? I mean Officer?"

Dewey took a sip of his coffee, and said, "Trying not to arrest you."

"Arrest me?" cried Toody. "For what!"

"The incident at the Country Club Saturday night."

"I have no clue to what you are referring."

"Well, I am not going to arrest you, even though it was suggested that I should arrest you and all the Daughters of Hernia. But you need to know that Brenda Jo Wyatt is suing you and The Daughters, the Country Club, the cow sponsors, and anybody she can think of that ruined her evening."

"Ruined her evening? Suing on what grounds? What in blue blazes are you talking about?"

"Well, let's see," Dew reached in his left pocket, pulled out his note pad and said, "Allegedly, you intentionally ruined her engagement party."

"Now just how in the name of the devil did I do that?" Toody asked.

Dew continued. "She claims the parking lot and sidewalk leading to and from the Country Club were littered with, let me see how she said it, 'bovine fecal matter.' She alleges that one of the tarps used for the cow plop was on the sidewalk of the Country Club causing her guests to have to either step on the tarp and or to try to step around it. It was difficult to see in the dark since the lights somehow were turned off.

Toody sipped her coffee and said, "The last time I saw the tarps they were being rolled up and taken to one of the trucks by the clean-up crew."

Deputy Dew Daah continued. "There is also the following: Destruction of property, creation of an unhealthy environment, and exceeding the number allotted parking spaces."

"How did I allegedly do that – the parking space thing?" Toody asked.

"You let the six contestants park their extraordinarily large and long cow trailers, in the front of the country club. Their pick-up trucks and trailers each took up about six parking places or 36 in all. Let's just round it up to 40 spaces."

"I was not in charge of parking that day. Go one," Toody replied.

The Deputy continued, "Alright, there is also: Littering, disturbing the peace with screaming and hollering, noise pollution with cow noises, air pollution arising from smells, mental harm to guests and individuals, and mental AND physical harm to Ms. Wyatt."

"How did I allegedly cause the physical harm to happen?" Toody asked.

"She turned her ankle when she stepped in pile of cow feces. Oh yes, she is suing for the cost of her dress and her shoes."

"Anything else?"

"Public embarrassment and mental distress to her. And she is trying to get that PETA organization to join the lawsuit for cow humiliation. Pooping in public."

"Well, I have no information about any of that," Toody said, pouring each one of them a second cup. "You were directing traffic that night. You saw me and the Daughters leave just after midnight. We were the last to leave beside the clean-up crew."

The Deputy continued. "A couple of funny things happened that night too. Seems the security cameras were not working that night for a couple of hours from about midnight to 2:00 AM. Something about a technology issue. And the sprinkler systems went off an hour early. They were supposed to automatically go off at 3:00 AM, but somehow, they went off at 2:00 AM just as Brenda Jo's guests were leaving."

Toody stared across the table. "I have no idea what happened after me, and the Daughters left. I do not know. Are you listening, Deputy?"

"What about the clean-up crew, Toody? Were they with the Country Club?"

"No," Toody smiled mysteriously. "They were just four very nice young men I found by the church shelter that morning. I paid cash on the barrel head for them to take the bucket of deposits and roll up the tarps and dispose of it all. As I have told you numerous times now, I do not know anything about it. Maybe the bucket where the deposits were placed after each round rolled off the truck. Perhaps one of the tarps fell from a truck."

Deputy Dewey Daah glared at Toody and said, "Toody? The tarp was partially unfurled and with edges taped to the sidewalk!"

Toody said, "Oh my goodness. Hmm."

The Deputy stood up to leave and just shook his head. He would probably never know what really happened that night.

As he was leaving, he turned to Toody and said, "Toody Byrd? You are one remarkable woman!"

At the following Tuesday Tex-Mex buffet at the Country Club, Deputy Dew found the ladies at their usual table, with their usual margaritas.

He approached the Daughters with a smile and said, "I just want y'all to know that Brenda Jo Wyatt dropped the charges this afternoon." Toody and the Daughters raised their glasses in celebration.

"Also thought you would like to know that she and Monty Heartherton eloped, and rumor has it that they are moving back to Houston."

Toody and the Daughters again raised their salt-rimmed glasses.

The Deputy smiled and said, "I'll be waiting to see you ladies home when you are ready," and walked away.

Toody and The Royal Order of the Daughters of Hernia raised their glasses high and Toody said, "La **vengeance** est un met que l'on doit manger froid." That is, "**Revenge** is a dish that must be **eaten cold**. And with a margarita and friends."

Dear Reader,

Did you enjoy They're Not Crazy – They're Southern? If you enjoyed it, please consider leaving an honest review on Amazon. Even if you did not enjoy it, leave an honest review on Amazon.

If (and when) typos, errors and/or mistakes are discovered, please send an email to deliaduffey@yahoo.com so I can correct.

Thank you,

Delia

17173050R00125